NIGHT SURFING

Fiona Capp was born in Melbourne in 1963. She currently works as a freelance writer and teaches fiction and journalism at RMIT. She trained as a journalist at *The Age* and has a PhD in English from La Trobe University. She is the author of *Writers Defiled: Security Surveillance of Australian Authors and Intellectuals 1920–1960* which was shortlisted for the FAW Australian Unity Literature Award in 1993.

NIGHT SURFING

FIONA CAPP

ALLEN & UNWIN

First published in 1996 by
Allen & Unwin Pty Ltd
9 Atchison Street, St Leonards, NSW 2065 Australia
Phone: (61 2) 9901 4088
Fax: (61 2) 9906 2218
E-mail: 100252.103@compuserve.com

Publication of this title was assisted by The Australia Council, the Federal Government's arts funding and advisory body.

National Library of Australia
Cataloguing-in-Publication entry:

Capp, Fiona.
  Night surfing.

  ISBN 1 86373 913 0.

  I. Title.

A823.3

Set in 10.5/14 pt Garamond by DOCUPRO, Sydney
Printed by Australian Print Group, Maryborough, Victoria

10 9 8 7 6 5 4 3

My thanks go to Sophie Cunningham for encouraging me to believe that there was a story to be told, and to Polly Crooke for making the editing a real pleasure.

Most of all I'd like to thank Steven Carroll whose example has taught me so much and whose advice has been invaluable.

To
Steven Carroll
and
Judith Wright

He thrust his joy against the weight of the sea;
climbed through, slid under those long banks of foam . . .
and swimming so, went out of sight
where mortal, masterful, frail, the gulls went wheeling
in air as he in water, with delight.

Turn home, the sun goes down; swimmer, turn home.
Last leaf of gold vanishes from the sea-curve.
Take the big roller's shoulder, speed and swerve;
come to the long beach home like a gull diving.

For on the sand the grey-wolf sea lies snarling . . .

— Judith Wright, 'The Surfer'

Mother, you had me
But I never had you . . .

— John Lennon, 'Mother'

PROLOGUE

IT BEGINS AS A ripple on the open ocean. Like a bullet travelling just below the skin of the water. The air about it hums and it registers as a slight judder under the hull of a passing ship. Way beneath the surface calm is a deep, far off rumble that seems to have no source. The horizon is clear; a tense thread in every direction.

The yet-to-be-born wave travels with great speed, a slight blip on the ocean's vast graph. In the glare of the noon sun that turns everything a blinding white, it is something felt not seen. A quiver that travels up through the feet. The trace of an invisible force racing across the ocean.

Towards late afternoon, a sea haze casts a dreamy spell over the water. In the still air is the memory of summers gone. As the ship steals on, the glassy water parts then closes behind, leaving streamers of tiny bubbles dissolving in its wake. Against the delicate blue of the sky and the denser ultramarine, it cuts a sharp profile as it noses towards the coast.

But far ahead, the ripple races on seeking a destination. A narrow spit of land looms, rigid and vulnerable. Thrust from the ochre cliffs, the worn face of the Sphinx watches its approach. As the ocean floor begins to shelve, the liquid shock wave compresses and has nowhere to go but up.

A vacuum is created. Like a deep inhalation before a thunderous sneeze, the water is sucked back from the Long Beach. The rock platform draped with weed and the sandy belly of the seabed are exposed. In the teeming rock pools, anemones sink deep into themselves and tiny fish flee into the crevices. For a brief moment, the sea holds its breath.

Then the water returns. A wave of colossal size towers over the dunes. A black wave that dredges up the sunless depths, a wave that arcs so high it drags down the sun, stars and moon from the sky and turns the day to pitch. Even the rotunda at the top of the cliff is swamped as thousands of tonnes of water come crashing over the land, ripping low scrub from the sandy earth and collapsing fibro houses like cards as it steams towards the town.

The wave is more than water. It carries a whole universe inside it. What is tossed up from the sea churns with the debris of the land as the inundation gains momentum. Shells, jellyfish, driftwood and deckchairs, bladder-wrack, corrugated iron, car tyres and starfish spiral down the deserted main street as Ruben's Cafe goes under, its neon lights still glowing beneath the water.

In the bank, the vault bursts open and the stored wealth of the town turns to instant mush. A siren blares from the fire brigade depot and then gurgles into silence. Mannequins from the drapers crash through the glass windows and bob up cloaked with weed. As the wave engulfs the whole town and finally spends itself in the bay, the only sign of what lies below is the limestone tower of the Continental Hotel rising above the surface, its shredded windsock flapping in surrender.

ONE

YOU HAD TO EXPECT some kind of damage—bruising, scars, a gash from the rocks perhaps. Hannah knew she couldn't come out of it untouched but she figured it would happen in the water and not on the road.

Something is thudding against the sides of the bus whenever the driver takes a corner too sharp or hits a dip in the road making everything lurch and come down hard. The suspension is shot but the driver doesn't seem to care. He knows his beast and he rides the bumps like a cowboy at home in the saddle.

She shouldn't have let him put it in the baggage compartment. It was custom-made for someone else who never came back, so she got it at a good price. Although it wasn't designed for her, its measurements suited a beginner. Fairly wide and not too short. Stable, in other words, the salesman said.

Hannah hangs on to the chrome rail attached to the seat in front and tries not to think about the damage. It hasn't been christened yet. She wanted to leave it at her feet or put it on the rack above the window but the driver insisted. 'No surfboards inside,' he said when the doors slapped open with a hiss and he saw her standing there, the sharp nose of it pointed at him like a torpedo. He heaved himself

7

down from his seat, opened the side of the bus and tossed it into the dark, empty space. It lay there wrapped in a stained old sheet that she'd rescued from her mother's rag bag. There was little else in the compartment to soften the blows if it slid around. She hadn't thought about foam packaging to protect it from the journey. Hannah had thought she could keep it with her. She didn't know there were rules about how surfboards could travel.

The gears crunch as the bus heads up Olivers Hill, leaving behind the flatlands of Frankston's housing commission estate as it climbs to Mt Eliza, winner of a Tidy Town award and a Tree Preservation Area; home of the new rich. Hannah looks back across the bay toward the city. A child's set of building blocks made pink by the dusk. At this point she is moving beyond its sprawling suburban edge. The train had taken her to the city's outer limits and now the final stage of the journey begins.

It has been a lost year.

Most of her friends spent their days in the pubs or cafes that lined the university end of town, but Hannah preferred the library where she could stare out the window, removed from it all, and dream about ways of escape. The university, with its old stone buildings, its spires and spacious lawns and air of well-bred ease, was too familiar for her liking. Everywhere, she recognised the faces of students from schools like her own. Schools where they had learned to believe that they were different from the rest. Little had changed that she could see. All she had done was move from a small cloister to a larger one with hardly a glimpse of what went on outside. She knew this world of bright

8

young things too well and it held no fascination for her. If this was having arrived, then for Hannah life was elsewhere.

Some days, when a hot northerly stirred up clouds of grit from between the tram tracks, she would skip tutorials and head for Flinders Street Station. She liked to listen to the departure announcements and smell the metallic whiff of the sea that came rushing out of the tunnels before a train drew into the platform.

All her life people had referred to her as the down to earth, sensible type. It was a description Hannah had come to fiercely resent. In school reports her teachers wrote approvingly that she had her feet 'planted on the ground'. What they didn't know was that this ground was constantly shifting; that *her* earth wasn't solid like theirs. She had no confidence in the ordered world that they, like her parents, took for granted. She was aware of movement, like sand running through her toes or the pull of a current underground that drew her toward the ocean. Those school reports should've read: She dreams of walking on water.

The bus rattles on toward the sea. Above the blue gums that line the highway the enormous screen of a drive-in flickers. A grainy, awe-struck face looms out of the darkness. The camera pans away to a crowd of people looking skyward where a tall building is engulfed in flames. Something is plummeting from the upper storeys, bright like a meteor until it crashes through a foyer canopy and on to the pavement. Hannah closes her eyes, remembering the first time she saw this movie and how she wanted to run from the cinema at the sight of the burning flesh.

As the road curves away, the Peninsula Drive-In is left behind and they continue through the coastal valley of grazing land and newly emerging wineries. The last part of the journey follows the bay. The land forms an arc like a crab's pincer, almost closing off the entrance to the open sea. At the mouth is the Rip where the water of the bay meets the ocean waves. Through this narrow opening only a few kilometres wide, the tides struggle for passage. Twice a day the waters break from the bay and surge into the ocean. Twice a day, like a birth in reverse, the ocean is sucked back into the bay. Hannah has heard many stories about the Rip—stories of motor boats dragged backward like toys and tankers forced to wait until the tide turns. Stories where all the radar equipment and sophisticated maps and channel markers count for nothing if the sea is too rough for the pilot boats to act as guides. Stories heightened by the remoteness of the Point which has been closed by the army for as long as she can remember.

Alongside the highway are retirement villages, holiday units and shopping complexes that front the bay. There are carnivals with Ferris wheels lit up against the night sky and the parted mouths of clowns turning slowly in their booths. There are dodgem cars and mini-golf and trampolines and Mr Whippy trucks playing Greensleeves mournfully slow. There are plenty of diversions on this pleasure strip but Hannah's attention is drawn to what lies hidden on the other side. There in the darkness, facing the South Pole, past the narrow stretch of bush, are the wind ravaged coastline and the violent waters of Bass Strait.

The bus stops at the top of her street. An unbroken

chain of headlights along the highway signals the beginning of the summer holidays. The driver opens the baggage compartment and has to reach into the far corner to retrieve her board. He drops it on the ground at her feet and before she has had a chance to inspect it, the bus is belching a cloud of exhaust as it pulls back on to the highway.

Hannah kneels on the gravel and gently tugs at the sheet as though teasing gauze from a wound. She runs her hands down the rails and feels their undented curves. Turning it over, she can almost see her face in the high gloss of the fibreglass. The fins are still firm and everything looks in order until she reaches the nose of the board which has clearly taken the brunt of all that lurching. Not only is it now snubbed, but the fibreglass has splintered and the white foam below is exposed like bone beneath the flesh.

Hannah wonders if she should try fixing it herself. If the ding isn't sealed it will become waterlogged and develop the dark, spreading bruises of second-hand boards. Carefully she wraps it up again. She picks up her carpet bag, tucks her board under one arm. Slowly she makes her way down the dirt track to the house. If she were brought here blindfolded she would know where she was from the smell of the tea-tree and the dusty corrugations beneath her feet.

Someone has left the outside light on. It casts a small pool of yellow over the front porch. In flowing wrought iron is the name of the house taken from a region of Scotland. The street is named after a city in Greece, the town itself after a coastal resort in Italy. Hannah likes these allusions to faraway places. The house is somewhere else. It's not her home but a place she escapes to, somewhere off the map of ordinary life. Even to spend her holidays behind the counter at Ruben's cafe is extraordinary. There she can be part of this other world and at the same time, be an observer of it.

He is the last one left in the water. It is dead flat. The tide is so full Jake will have to go out past Darby's Rock to find anything resembling a wave. Aware that he is being watched, he leans back and swings the nose of his board toward the shore. The others are in the carpark above the beach. Tim has his wetsuit half-off and is rubbing his hair with an orange towel. Sam is hopping on one foot with his head cocked. On the bonnet of the ute is Louie, hands cupped around his mouth, hooting madly. They want him to go drink with them. They can't understand what keeps him out there when there is no swell. Jake lifts an arm, salutes and turns away. He hears the car start up and when the hum of the motor fades he begins stroking out toward the horizon.

Before Jake came to the Peninsula he had never seen the surf. All he knew were the Liverpool docks, the outline of cranes and containers stacked on the wharves. Only tankers and ferries rode the Irish Sea, not men on planks of foam and fibreglass. Merseysiders were pale and did not go in the water which was sick with chemicals and industrial waste. He had never given the surf a second thought until his father got it into his head that pain could be left behind if you went far enough away. When his father first mentioned going south, Jake thought of Lands End where his parents had spent their honeymoon. His father looked scornful. 'Don't be daft, boy.' Marcus hated Southerners.

From the high diving tower at the Mersey council pool, the aqua rectangle below was mesmerising. This was the water Jake loved. Utterly contained and still. The first time he achieved a forward dive with a pike, touching his toes mid-air and then squaring-out to meet the pool head on, it seemed that anything was possible. One year later, just as they were to leave the country, he discovered how to launch himself like a crucifix and twist around so that he faced the direction from which he had come. It was a difficult move and his father was proud, but the demands of training were already beginning to tell. Although he would not have admitted it to anyone, it came as a relief when he had to leave it all behind.

What Jake remembered about the flight was the sight of Lake Geneva, a tiny lozenge of water surrounded by the Alps. He imagined himself diving toward it, his body plummeting like a missile and then the smallest of splashes as he disappeared from view. He'd slept after that as they flew into the night. He woke hours later as they were crossing a flat plain with rivers snaking through it. Soon the rivers petered out and the soil grew redder. Out of nowhere there was a massive rock, completely alone. The pilot made an announcement and everybody flocked to the left side of the plane. When they finally got to the

13

small coastal town where Jake and his father were to live, he didn't know which way was up.

He stops paddling and rolls off his board. His body disappears. Below him the sea floor is shadowy with rock and kelp. He likes to be alone in the water when it's like this. Nothing but the occasional surge travelling to shore. No pressure to hassle for waves, no need to perform. The beach is empty. A lone figure leans from the rotunda at the top of the bluff.

The sun is slipping into the sea. The wind has dropped. A big moon, thin as tissue paper, is rising over the dunes. When Anton gets back from his desert trek, he and Jake will go surfing by moonlight. They'll wait until the moon is full and then build a fire in the dunes to mark their position by. They'll pad across the cool sand and with one easy motion glide into the liquid darkness. Jake has never been out after dusk. From the cliff tops he has seen the streaks of luminous foam but they always look like phantom waves, impossible to catch. Anton says it's like riding on air.

Anton had been Jake's teacher. He'd taught him science and he'd taught him how to surf. Even now that the pupil had surpassed his master Jake remained in Anton's thrall. Anton had seen Jake through his initiation and had a hold on him that Jake barely understood. Anton forgot nothing and could recount Jake's progress and make it sound like an epic. He remembered Jake's first cut back, re-entry, tube and above all, the three-sixty that saw him whirl like a dervish in a shower of spray during the big Easter swells of '73. Anton told it like a story that placed Jake at the centre of things and foreshadowed glorious days.

After school, whenever the conditions were right, Anton and his coterie of blond-haired boys would march, boards under their arms, down the Ocean Beach Road to the Back Beach. A procession of excited faces with zinc cream smeared like war paint across their noses. Little warriors off to do battle with Hughie, the vengeful god of the waves.

Jake was a natural on the water and Anton saw it straight away. He had the poise and control of the diver but he also knew how to position himself to catch the wave. He paddled sideways into it, not riding it straight down like a slide as most of the boys did. He understood how subtle shifts of weight and posture made all the difference. There was something else, unrelated to talent. His recklessness. Most beginners spent their time dodging waves, duck-diving under them, forever awash in the shorebreak. They progressed slowly from the whitewater to the soft shoulder of the diminishing wave. But Jake was too impatient and would rather take a pounding than bide his time. He was out the back with the older surfers almost as soon as he could paddle the distance.

Jake and Anton would fall in together as they made their way to the beach: the teacher with the polio-stunted legs and the boy trailing his leg-rope like a leash. Anton was a fund of stories and facts about surfing, the tides and the pull of the moon. The land had tides, he told Jake. But the earth's solid crust made the motion so slight that no one was aware of it happening. And even the smallest body of liquid had a tidal range: a glass of beer or a bowl of soup, if you could somehow measure it. Jake didn't know what to think when Anton said things like that. He would stare at him, unsure whether to laugh. Sometimes Anton would ruffle his hair and look preoccupied, sometimes he would grin and say, 'What d'you reckon about that?' And Jake would be at a loss again.

From the roundabout Jake can see that Ruben's is closed. The blinds are down and the umbrellas are gone from the tables outside. The Holden slides over the gravel and he lets the engine idle while he tries the door. He pushes his face to the glass. Through the dark interior the stainless steel benchtops gleam. The deep-fry is off. There's a soft neon glow in the deli counter. On the tables the chairs are stacked, their legs in the air. Jake thumps his palm against the door making the CLOSED sign jiggle and go skew-whiff.

After a long pause a tall figure in a long, white apron moves out from behind a rack of chips and crackers. He might have been there all the time, just watching to see what Jake would do. Ruben often lingered by the windows with a spatula or broom in hand as though frozen mid-action by thoughts of somewhere else, somewhere far from the greasy fumes of hamburgers, burnt milk and deep fried batter. His drooping moustache and hooded grey eyes added to this forlorn impression.

But Jake knew that thoughts of escape weren't what stopped Ruben in his tracks.

Jake stomps his feet on the paving to loosen the sand before going inside. For those whom Ruben favors, the cafe is never closed. They sit together at one of the tables while Ruben refills the salt and pepper shakers and talks of his plans to sell up once the summer is over. Jake looks over his jaffa milkshake and licks the foam that clings to his lips. His face glowing from the day in the sun. His hair is still wet. He has heard this talk before and doesn't believe it. Ruben is proud of his cafe and the business he has built up out of the rundown corner milkbar it had been.

Jake can remember how it was before Ruben's. There was nowhere to go but the pubs. They were alright for a drink but they weren't near the beach and besides, the food was terrible. Then Ruben and Marie came along and recognised what was needed. A place for the kids to go after school, for the locals to meet for a coffee and smoke; for the surfers to gather after a day in the water. It had become Jake's second home.

'You've been saying that for years,' Jake says. He wishes Ruben would snap out of it.

'This time it's serious,' Ruben says. Marie is so restless it frightens him. She's sick of studying by correspondence. She wants to be on campus full-time. She wants the student life she never had at eighteen. To Ruben it's the beginning of the end.

'I can see it coming. Once she gets that piece of paper she'll go. What would keep her here?'

'The food?'

'Don't be funny. You should see her on Tuesdays. She can't wait to get out the door.'

Ruben digs a teaspoon into a bowl of sugar, lifts it high and lets the fine grains fall through the air. Jake watches

Ruben hunched over the table top and realises that he has never seen him outside the cafe.

Jake doesn't know what to advise. Since his mother died, his father hasn't seemed interested in other women. It's all a mystery to him, this business of communicating. For over a decade it has been just the two of them. At twenty-three Jake knows how to fuck a woman but not how to talk to her.

'Look,' he says finally. 'There's a dead fly.'

Ruben flicks it from the sugar bowl and smiles to himself.

'They get into everything. You wouldn't believe the places I find them.'

The hot water has run cold but Marie doesn't move. She has been under the shower for the length of a symphony and has no desire to get out. A voice from the radio tells her it was Mozart in G minor. She examines her hands. The tips of her fingers are spongy and white. The plughole is blocked with Cherry Ripe and Picnic wrappers and water is beginning to slosh around her ankles. Half a Mars Bar pokes from her mouth. Sometimes she just can't stop, even to wash her hair. The soapy water streams over her slightly rounded belly and slim thighs.

When she's serving the tables she doesn't notice the food. It has no power over her. All she sees is muck on a plate that customers pay money for and then shovel into their mouths. Marie has tossed out too many half-eaten pies, scraps of beef in gravy, and chips drenched in vinegar to desire the food that Ruben cooks. She works without eating. In the evening she's exhausted and flakes out on the loungeroom floor with her feet propped up on the sofa.

Sometimes, as she watches the blades of the ceiling fan turn in lazy, endless circles, she thinks of how another day has slipped her by. She is forty-five and she once had plans. Plans that didn't involve twelve hours a day behind a fast food counter. By this time of evening her blood sugar is low and her stomach is knotted and empty. Through the doorway that leads to the shop she spies the chocolate bars glittering in their wrappers. Her life might be on hold but some pleasure can be salvaged.

The bingeing began when she was thirteen years old and newly in the thrall of forbidden desires. Every year in the country town where she was born, girls not much older than herself would disappear to the city overnight, spirited away by their parents until their swelling bodies had returned to their normal shape. No longer 'with child' they would come back home as though nothing had happened, their lips forever sealed. But many of them never returned and rumours circulated that served to chasten the young girls of the town.

When Marie's time came to make the long journey, it was to work as a stenographer in a big city mining firm, and hers was a public farewell. She wore her new twin-set and waved a gloved hand at family and friends who stood on the platform. After the conductor had passed through and checked her ticket, she put her feet up on the seat opposite. Stretching out her legs, she watched the countryside float by. She didn't care if she never saw another field of wheat again in her life. Her hands rested on her plump belly and in her lap was a tin of chocolate hedgehog her mother had made for the journey. As the day grew hotter, she stuck her head out the window and felt the rush of cool air on her face. Later, in the toilet cubicle at the end of the carriage, she leaned back against the door as it swayed, and watched the half-digested hedgehog disappear down the silver gullet.

For all her determination never to return to that town, she finds herself, almost thirty years on, in another small town longing for what the city holds. The ocean has replaced the wheat fields but little else has changed. Her days are spent serving food, just as her mother's and her grandmother's were before her. She mightn't cook but the old rituals prevail. It's Ruben's cafe and she is the waitress.

Waiting. Always waiting. Apart from the money, what has she been waiting for? All the energy she and Ruben might've put into love has gone into the cafe. Their days have been spent waiting on strangers rather than satisfying themselves. A gauntness in both their faces tells of a hunger that won't go away.

It was only two months after she arrived at the Spencer Street terminus in 1951 that Marie had met Ruben. She was living with her aunt at the time. One day the door chime went and standing on the porch was a lanky figure in a well-cut suit with a vacuum cleaner in each hand. He had two models, a barrel type with a long tube that you dragged along behind you and an upright that looked like it could drive itself. He tipped a paperbag full of dirt on to a sample piece of carpet and instructed her to watch. He said things about 'superior suction' and 'durability' but halfway through his spiel he caught her looking at him strangely and lost track of what came next. The more

Marie smiled, the more embarrassed he became. He stumbled on, blushing deeply until he finally ground to a halt. He had a confession to make, he told her. He hated his job. He hated knocking on strangers' doors and being at their mercy. He hated repeating himself a hundred times a day. He hated life on the road and getting chased by dogs. He hated the whole routine.

He was packing up by now and Marie wondered if this was part of the act. Perhaps he sold lots of machines this way. Marie wasn't going to be fooled. She would help him put the pieces away in their boxes and then she'd say goodbye. When she saw how flustered he'd become she offered to help him carry them back to his car but this seemed to alarm him more. All the time he kept glancing back at the street. Marie grabbed the nearest box and marched out to the footpath. But the street was empty. A few houses up, partially hidden behind a tree was a motorbike, its sidecar full of boxes.

Ruben was beyond caring now and led the way. He dumped the rest of the machines in the sidecar, took off his suit coat and pulled on a cracked leather jacket over his waistcoat.

'You're not supposed to see this,' he said, lowering his helmet. 'The boss thinks it's bad for the company's image.'

Marie stared at him—the bulky jacket, the gleaming chrome exhaust, the tight leather gloves, the eyes like Ned Kelly's. He had meant what he'd said. It wasn't a pose. She knew what they'd think of him back home and this made her want him more.

'That's a fine looking bike,' Marie said, although she didn't know a thing about them.

Ruben threw his leg over it and eased on to the seat. He gripped the handlebars.

'It's a Harley Panhead,' he said proudly. 'Latest model.'

Marie told him she knew how he felt. Her first job was in phone sales but she'd only lasted two days. She had a bad habit of laughing in the middle of her pitch.

'My aunt could really do with one of those cleaners,' she said. Anything to bring him back. 'She uses a straw broom for heaven's sake. Why don't you come round tomorrow morning. She'll be here then.'

Less than a year later they were married and Marie moved from one family home to another. It felt like a smooth transition, like good domestic management to find herself married at the age of seventeen. A few years later, Ruben put away his leather jacket, retired the Harley Davidson, and bought a station wagon. It was his way of saying that he wanted to start a family. It gave Marie a fright because she wasn't ready for children and wondered if she ever would be. Looking back, she couldn't help feeling that things had started to go wrong from there.

Then eventually Marie began studying again and after that, everything changed. She couldn't look at the world in the same way. At school, her idea of learning had been to worship at the feet of the great and to absorb the wisdom of the ages. But now she saw that awe made her mind seize up. To be enthralled was to be a slave. Only when she was prepared to question would she ever really learn. Only when she let go of her old certainties would she discover the kind of knowledge she'd always been searching for.

22

Ruben wipes the sauce that has oozed from the nozzle of the large plastic tomato. He has five of them lined up in front of him like a row of prize-winning exhibits. He polishes their bright red rumps, and thinks of Marie. She has started raiding the shop at all hours. He tries to speak to her about it, but she doesn't seem to hear. She even eats in bed while reading a book or doing a crossword. Crumbs of wafer and chocolate fall around her on the sheets and he might as well not exist. Afterwards he hears her in the bathroom. He doesn't know which is worse—the way she stuffs her face, or the sound of her throwing up afterwards.

'She's got a problem with food,' Ruben is saying to Jake when Marie bursts through the saloon doors. Ruben jolts around, afraid he's been overheard.

Marie has a bottle of champagne in one hand and three glasses in the other. Her hair is dripping from the shower. She carefully places the glasses in front of them and smiles at Jake. She removes the foil letting the cork fly across the room where it bounces on the tiled floor. Vapor rises from the mouth like a genie finally let loose. Sitting at the end of the table she raises her glass.

'Her name is Hannah,' she announces and sips her drink, blinking as the bubbles fizz in her nose. She has convinced Ruben they need help in the cafe this summer. Since they came to the town ten years ago they have worked on their own. The hours have been long; the cafe open seven days a week.

'For the first time in years, I'm going to lie on the beach and read.' She eyes her husband. 'And Ruben might even step outside.'

23

Marie smiles again at Jake. She is thinking about the summer and beyond it to the university year when she will once again sit in those draughty lecture halls with her notebook in front of her. She knows exactly what she wants now and it has made all the difference. The smallest things infuriate her, like Ruben's quiet, unhurried manner around the cafe; the way he loiters at the window staring at nothing. As though he had all the time in the world—as though time were not running out.

At the end of the day she can't bear to watch him clean up. He always wipes everything twice. One evening, just before closing time when he was out the back unpacking frozen chickens from the delivery van, Marie scoured the deep-fry and washed down the windows. Half an hour later, after locking up, she watched him blindly wipe them over as though the ritual had to be performed, regardless of the need.

'So who's this Hannah?' says Ruben.

'Not a local, I bet,' mutters Jake.

'I met her in zoology. We were dissecting a rat.'

'Of course,' says Ruben, 'where else would you find a waitress?'

TWO

EVERY MORNING MARCUS PARKS the Dodge at London Bridge and smokes a roll-your-own while listening to the news. From the clifftop he can see two kilometres up the beach to where the Sphinx thrusts her eroded profile into the Strait. He examines the surf and sees it through Jake's eyes—which sandbanks are producing the cleanest waves, how the wind is sculpting the swell, where the rips are working, which way the tide is flowing.

He likes to watch the haze lift. At first the sea rolls in out of nowhere and the far end of the beach is lost in whiteness. Slowly the veils are lifted and the lifesavers' club house emerges, a grey cube propped on stilts in the high dunes. Further on, there are fishermen with buckets at their feet and rods jammed into the sand. From the way the tip of the rod curves forward he can imagine the line cast into the shorebreak to form a triangle. When he has the time, he waits for the distant outline of Cape Schanck to appear, marking the end of the territory he patrols for the National Parks.

From under the tarpaulin Marcus takes a spike and a hessian bag and treads the limestone steps to the sand. The beach has that washed-out look it gets after a storm when the waves have surged high up to finger the dunes, scattering debris as they retreat. He lunges at a milk carton and then at a cola can, storing up rubbish on the spike until it can take no more. The motion has become as automatic as hoisting the bins to his shoulder was back home. Soon the hessian bag rattles as he walks.

Along the high tide line there is something brown and round. He tests it carefully with his foot. A jet of water shoots into the air. Closer, he sees the separate sacs of the sea squirt bunched together like grapes. He is tempted to prod it again and watch it spray or even to jump on it and hear it pop. Instead he scoops it into his backpack. His job has made a beachcomber of him.

In Liverpool he was 'on the bins'. A bin man. He combed the streets. Now the landscape has changed. When Jake was much younger, he told his friends that his father was a sandman. The National Parks call him something official but it makes no difference to Marcus. He has become a connoisseur of debris, live and dead, man-made and natural, organic and inorganic. Most of the man-made goes in his bag and then to the hopper to be squashed into massive bricks of waste and incinerated. Sometimes he might find a dead Fairy penguin or a Sooty albatross tangled in bladder-wrack or netting. These he takes to the ranger for further investigation. The rest goes in his pack to be sorted later. One of his greatest finds is a whale ear bone—a hollow structure the shape of a kidney and the size of his palm. Somehow it had got dislodged from the skull. Not that many years before a whole herd of sperm whales had beached themselves further up the coast.

It is a cleaner job than working the bins but Marcus misses the jokes with the men, the paved streets and the sooty brick terraces as they begin to stir. On the beach he is aware of other stirrings, but most are unconnected with human activity. Only gradually have the words he has learned—the names for what he collects or hopes to collect—made familiar this strange landscape. Creatures called seadragons, shells called argonauts, sponge called dead man's fingers. Layers of myth that weave the skeletons and carapaces of the oceans into human history. It has forced him to think about the cycles that bring him this flotsam of the sea.

Not long ago there had been a Catholic school excursion from the city. It was a blowy, unsettling afternoon with a cool change forecast. The lifesavers were on duty and the children kept between the flags but no one had noticed the littoral current that cut right through the safe zone and connected with a rip travelling out to the open sea. Before anyone knew what had happened, a boy was dragged beyond the shorebreak, his cries muffled by the booming surf. When they spotted him from the lookout he was no longer thrashing. He bobbed at the surface for a while before disappearing. Then the red of his bathers was seen further out. White-faced teachers counted the rest of the children and quick-marched them up the cliff. All necks craned back towards the ocean. By the time the lifesavers' dinghy had powered its way across the breakers, he was gone.

The flags were crossed to signal that the beach was closed. Even the fishermen reeled in their lines, afraid perhaps, of what they might catch.

Marcus found him at the Back Beach, a small bay north-east of the Long Beach. The day after the boy disappeared Marcus saw something as he drove the Dodge down the hill to the carpark. As he ran along the beach, his boots grew heavy with water and sand. There was a large natural rock pool with an outer rim of tinted concrete—a local council project to make it safe for children. The boy was floating there on his stomach the way that Jake used to do when he went diving with his mask and snorkel. The high tide, that flushed the stagnant pool with the teeming water of the ocean, had washed him in.

Marcus's eyes were stinging as he waded into the pool. He looked back towards the carpark. There was no one else around. He knew he would have to do it. Cradle the boy in his arms and lift him out.

After that he started having dreams more disturbing than anything he thought himself capable of imagining. They weren't frightening like childhood nightmares. They were more impersonal than that. They were more like visions of annihilation by a force utterly indifferent to life. A mindless, awesome force that once set in motion could never be stopped. A deep, nagging unease would hang over him for days afterwards. Sometimes months could go by without another episode, but as soon as he dared to think that he was free of it, the dreams would always return.

It begins as a ripple on the open ocean. Like a bullet travelling just below the skin of the water. The air about it hums and it registers as a slight judder under the hull of a passing ship. Way beneath the surface calm is a deep, far off rumble that seems to have no source. The horizon is clear, a tense thread in every direction.

The yet-to-be-born wave travels with great speed, a slight blip on the ocean's vast graph. In the glare of the noon sun that turns everything a blinding white, it is something felt not seen. A quiver that travels up through the feet. The trace of an invisible force racing across the ocean.

It is late afternoon and a sea haze casts a dreamy spell over the water. In the still autumn air is the memory of summers gone. As the ship steals on, the glassy water parts then closes behind, leaving streamers of tiny bubbles dissolving in its wake. Against the delicate blue of the sky and the denser ultramarine, it cuts a sharp profile as it noses towards the coast.

But far ahead, the ripple races on seeking a destination. A narrow spit of land looms, rigid and vulnerable. Thrust from the ochre cliffs, the worn face of the Sphinx watches its approach. As the ocean floor begins to shelve, the liquid shock wave compresses and has nowhere to go but up.

A vacuum is created. Like a deep inhalation before a thunderous sneeze, the water is sucked back from the Long Beach. The rock platform draped with weed and the sandy belly of the seabed are exposed. In the teeming rock pools, anemones sink deep into themselves and tiny fish flee into the crevices. For a brief moment, the sea holds its breath.

Then the water returns.

THREE

THE NEXT MORNING HANNAH wakes to the sound of the weatherboard ticking under the early morning sun and a possum leaping on the iron roof. Claws scrabble and then silence. Liquid patches of blue, green and red swim on the walls from the stained glass transparency she has stuck to the window. Above her bed is a sepia poster of the perfect wave. The shoulder is thick. The face of it like glass. The lip curves over to form a hollow that frames the tropical shore behind. It is poised and shimmering. It will never break.

Hannah drags her shorts over her bathers and lets the wire door slam behind her. She walks barefoot across the couch grass in the front yard. When she reaches the gravel at the side of the road she pulls her runners on. She takes short cuts through lanes where the ivy has run wild and formed canopies across the tea-tree. She jogs down the centre of the deserted main street, where the tram used to run from the pier at the turn of the century. Near the bank is a noticeboard with a map for tourists. There is a black dot marked on the grid of streets. YOU ARE HERE. She passes through a sweet smelling cloud from the bakery. An open-sided truck is dropping off its load of daily papers at the newsagent which has just opened. Next door, above the milkbar and grocery store, the vanilla top of the giant Streets icecream is melting under the early morning sun.

Finally she leaves the township behind and heads into a light on-shore wind down the Ocean Beach Road. She plunges into the foreshore track and on to the Long Beach where the air has the rotten tang of dried seaweed. The low tide has exposed a wide platform at the base of the Sphinx. There is something naked about it. All those sharp edges of rock and pools that she had forgotten were there.

She runs on the firm sand close to the water. When she looks back she sees that her footsteps have created a series of arcs from where she has skirted the waves. She cartwheels and her hand prints break up the pattern. Hannah moves easily through the air. She's been running all her life.

At primary school she was known as a sprinter and her father believed that, with coaching, she could be a champion. On Saturdays she went in competitions where the parents barracked furiously from the sidelines and the children collapsed sobbing at the finish. After school she would practise crouching at the starting blocks, waiting for the crack of the gun. But then her arms began to tremble and she sensed that something wasn't right. She'd just turned twelve when her body confirmed her suspicions. The spurt of early growth that'd given her an edge, came to a sudden halt. She began to fill out. Her breasts seemed to weigh her down. Her arms and legs grew thicker. She got stronger at long distance and lost her speed.

Her father refused to see it, and when she stopped winning he stepped up the training. He'd stand right behind her as she settled into the blocks and tell her it was all in the mind. Imagine a dark street late at night, he would say. She was walking down the broken white line. There was no one else around. The street lights were out. Ahead of her was nothing but darkness. Behind her there were footsteps. Heavy and deliberate. They were getting closer. She knew what they meant. She could freeze or she could run. Go, he'd suddenly bark, and Hannah would fly from the blocks, her heart thumping in her ears.

Hannah stopped training after that. She couldn't tell her father why. As a boy he'd dreamed of the Olympic Games and the roar of the crowd as he broke the tape. One summer when he was seventeen, he was swinging like Tarzan across the wide, brown Yarra when the rope snapped above a submerged log and his dreams ended with a crook back. In the photographs Hannah had seen of his sporting days, he was all toothy smiles and loose limbs. Holding a trophy aloft or sprawling on the grass after a race, his eyes were triumphant. In the days that followed his injury, he did something that amazed every-one who knew him—he asked for the school chaplain. When Michael emerged from his hospital bed, he'd decided to enter the church.

All her life they had lived in the eastern suburban vicarage with its cottage garden and privet hedge. Staked roses, expertly pruned, lined the pathway to the front door. In their tree-lined street, all the houses were old and had high walls. The place had a solid, imperturbable air and in the summer months the only sound of life was the cicadas in the empty streets. It was the most desolate sound Hannah knew. Sometimes it would be tempered by the swelling notes of the organ. Her mother, Alice, practised in the church every afternoon. She always finished with 'Jesu Joy of Man's Desiring' which seemed to go on forever, the melody dying in one voice only to be taken up by another. Alice and Michael worked as a team; a united front.

Some things were still hard to reconcile. The mild-faced Anglican minister, and the man who'd told her to run for her life.

Above the usual sounds of the sea there is music. At first just a rhythmic pulse, snatches of a brassy tune and the background crackle of loudspeakers. From the club house in the dunes, Hannah sees two columns of lifesavers in crimson speedos and yellow and red caps, marching down to the shoreline. The front four carry a reel and line. Those following shoulder a large wooden boat as though it were a coffin. A voice barks and someone from the back of the column runs to the water's edge and dives headlong in. When he has swum beyond the shorebreak, he raises an arm as though drowning. At this signal, the boat is launched and a man harnessed to the line plunges into the waves.

They are still in order, barracking with fists in the air as Hannah jumps the sand-drenched rope. Their bodies are well-shaped and brown, shoulders and thighs bulging from running in the dunes and knifing through the waves. The younger ones are slighter. Their faces have familiar soft features, like the boys she knew at the grammar school. At cadet training they wore stiff khaki and did drills around the quadrangle. Their jaws locked tightly together. Their chins thrust out and shoulders pulled back.

A shrill whistle silences them. The harnessed lifesaver is being reeled in with the drowning man resting against him. The surf boat has been upturned by the waves and the men are trying to right it. As Hannah passes, a voice calls from the balcony of the clubhouse. It is one of those soft-faced boys. He looks familiar. She raises a hand and keeps on running.

The beach opens out in front of her. Hannah moves toward a solitary figure in the distance. She can just make out a man in a green Parks uniform bending over a mound of kelp. The sand shudders with her steps and the man looks up, surprised. He watches her pass. Near London Bridge, where the waves explode under the arch in the rock, Hannah stops running and sits for a while to catch her breath. Leaning back on her elbows, she makes canals with her heels in the sand.

The forecast was for a northerly but the high pressure system still hovers in the Bight and a south-easterly prevails. Jake, Sam and Louie have been at the Long Beach since dawn but their boards remain strapped to Jake's car. Every morning they buy the paper to check the weather map and tide times. Their days are governed by highs and lows and approaching fronts. In the evenings they tune into the television news just to get the weather. When the giant map comes on to the screen, they turn up the volume, their eyes fixed on the isobars. They know that winter is the best time for powerful ground swell produced by lows in the Bight and driven between the two Capes. This time of year the swell is wind-forced and the waves die quickly when the wind drops away.

Harry's food van has just opened in the carpark. Jake orders a hamburger for breakfast and eats it distractedly as he leans on the fence. The on-shore wind has made a mess of everything. Waves sputter and die all over the place. Out the back, long lines of foam steam in and flatten everything before them. If there was just one sandbank working Jake would give it a go but not even Sam, who will try anything, can be bothered. Jake rattles the wire fence as though it were the only thing holding him back. In these conditions only Quarantine Station works. But Louie's father is out fishing so they have no boat to get there.

Jake is considering the options when a brass band starts up from the club house below. He shouts to the others and they crowd the lookout to see the lifesavers parading down the beach. Louie falls in with the beat and starts goose-stepping across the bitumen. He turns, clicks his heels and his arm snaps out. Sam returns the gesture and they march toward each other like clockwork soldiers. They are strutting and crying 'Heil Clubbie' when a white Rolls Royce appears over the hill and cruises slowly down. Sam and Louie stand to attention and salute as though greeting a head of state. From behind the wheel a middle-aged man frowns and guides the Rolls once around the carpark before disappearing back over the hill.

Jake kicks at the dirt and wipes the grease from his fingers down his jeans. He looks across at Louie and Sam. He tilts his nose into the air and does the voice he remembers from the BBC news. It was never hard to pick the ones from the mansions overlooking the bay. Jake hates the way they flaunt themselves. They acted as if they were the locals and the town were theirs. They spoke in precise, slightly drawled voices and ordered seafood vol-au-vents by the dozen at Harry's. The sons joined the lifesaving club and patrolled the beach. The daughters were so confident they frightened him. They wore ribbons in their hair, designer jeans with baggy jumpers and laughed like Marilyn Monroe. Their parents wore American loafers, long shorts and striped sailor shirts. They all sported deep, even tans. To Jake they were another species.

Sometimes gossip columnists from the tabloid papers came sniffing around for stories about the summer parties these people held. One time, Louie's father told them a story about floating brothels that cruised the bay. He explained how boats made calls to the private jetties at the exclusive end of town. Masked women, and boys dressed in togas, had been seen climbing the limestone steps of the cliff. They were ushered through security gates and into the high-walled gardens beyond. After servicing the mansions along the coast, the pleasure boats would plough through the darkness to the army barracks at the tip of the peninsula where business was brisk. By the time the horizon had turned pink they were motoring back to the docks.

The Establishment families kept to themselves as they had done for over a hundred years. At the local museum, Jake had seen old tourist brochures from the turn of the century that advertised the local attractions. It was known as a summer playground for the affluent.

Not long after he and his father came to live in the town, Jake noticed what looked like battlements rising above the bush behind London Bridge. They were visible only from certain spots before sinking into the surrounding vegetation. Sometimes he wondered if he had imagined them. For many years he thought they belonged to a monastery.

One afternoon, when he was about thirteen and the ocean was as flat as a brick, he began walking in the direction of the towers. He made his way over back fences, across a golf course and forced a path through the tea-tree scrub which swallowed the horizon with a blanket of green. The distance was further than it looked and he was thinking of turning back when the bush started to give way, taking on the appearance of a cultivated estate with great pines, cypresses, lemon scented gums and a miniature maze. A massive edifice filled the blue sky—a castle of roughly hewn limestone with Roman arches and Tudor ramparts and imposing square towers. There was a garage towards the back the size of a large house with what looked like servants' quarters above it. It might have been there for centuries but he knew that wasn't possible. At the base of a peppercorn tree he found a brass plaque, a memorial to the wealthy grazier who had built the castle in the 1930s. He had died only nine months after its completion.

Jake roamed around the grounds, moving from shadows to sunshine and back again. As he approached the walls he felt a chill coming from them. The day was muggy yet the stones were cold. He passed the hothouse where fat, tropical flowers pressed their faces against the glass; passed the folly with jasmine tumbling strategically over the Doric columns; passed the outhouses made to look like rustic stables; passed the fountain where Neptune cavorted with mermaids, the water spurting from the prongs of his trident into the pool below. It was like something from a book. He couldn't imagine real people living there.

A light breeze travelled across the lawn. The tops of the pines bent away from the Strait and Jake wondered if the cool change would pick up the swell. He followed the pathway around to the front again. Everything was familiar and yet bizarrely out of place. Castles were no big deal back home. They seemed to be everywhere. His father had always scoffed at their pretentious grandeur and the nostalgia they inspired for some mythical, idealised past. Yet this cool appraisal clashed with his memory of the stories his mother used to tell him before bed. Stories of knights and slayings, unicorns and hermits, maidens and dragons. Things not of this world. Stories with the magical power to conjure up her voice.

Jake sighed and blinked into the sun. A figure was emerging from the shade of the cloisters and was crossing the lawn toward him. He was pushing a wheelbarrow and calling out something. Although the voice was harsh and angry it took Jake some seconds to register that it was directed at him. He waited as the figure kept coming, wanting to tell him that he had done nothing wrong. He was just looking around.

When the man started brandishing a rake, Jake saw that it was pointless. He turned and bolted like a thief down the wide driveway, the gravel crunching loudly under foot. Either side were cypresses with great dark wings that blocked out the sky. The driveway ended at a wrought iron gate that was locked. There were brass crosses on the concrete posts and barbed-wire above the high stone wall. With a running jump he leapt and held the wire down with his hand as he scrambled over. At the road he stuck out his thumb and walked in a kind of trance until the local fruiterer pulled over and gave him a ride into town.

Afterwards, Jake sat in the kiosk at the top of the hill and stared out over the Norfolk pines to the bay beyond. It was chopped and silvery in the late afternoon light. At the pier, the ferry was backing up. Water churned around the pylons. A drawbridge was lowered so the cars could drive straight off. One by one they rolled back on to the land, the family station wagons, the BMWs, the kombi vans, the Mercedes, the hatch-backs, the sports cars, the Jaguars, the utes. Most took the road that curved up the hill past the kiosk.

Before they reached the top Jake knew which direction they would take. The expensive cars turned right toward *that* end of town. The others went straight ahead toward the shopping centre, the fibro holiday shacks and the camping grounds. Once he started looking for them, the signs were everywhere. The signs of difference that every-one seemed determined to deny. Jake sipped his drink and held an angry conversation with himself. He could still hear the gardener's voice. It made him want to smash something.

He became one of those gardeners himself, for a brief time in his eighteenth year. After leaving school just before the fifth form exams, he had tried a series of short term jobs—laboring with the National Parks during the summer, helping out a friend in his roofing business, working on the council road gang, even delivering letters for a while until his habit of disappearing when there was a northerly put an end to that. For months his father had been on his back about getting a job and gardening was the kind of work that would give him time to surf.

He had never been inside one of the big summer houses. Little was evident to those who passed by on the road. It was only from the water that their dominance of the landscape could be appreciated. Great limestone structures laced with balconies and surrounded by green lawn that sloped all the way to the cliff edge. Or Edwardian facades with turrets, elaborate fretwork and verandahs like moats. Or modern boxes of glass stacked at strange angles with wide sundecks and spotlighted tennis courts. Some had private beaches, others had rocky escarpments. Yachts and boats of all sizes were moored in the waters below.

Jake had been hoping that the garden would be native but he knew the chances weren't good. Anything built before 1960 would be English style with a million flower beds to weed and roses to prune and hedges to trim and little grottos to keep neatly shambling. When he rolled up at 'Quincey Hall' he found it had all this and more. The town had been the first settlement in the State (the pioneers had quickly changed their minds and gone else-where) and 'Quincey' was one of its oldest buildings. The foundation stones had been laid by the convicts who were brought to clear the land before the settlement was abandoned. When Jake got the job, the caretaker showed him around the grounds like a guide leading a tourist through an historic homestead.

It was early summer—he had been working there for just over a month—and he was cleaning the leaves from the swimming pool in preparation for the family's arrival. The caretaker never called them by their names so he only knew them as 'the family'. He was standing at the edge in his overalls, delving into the green water with a net. There was a fine layer of brown mulch suspended over the bottom. He was thinking about when he used to go diving, about the rush before take-off and how his body felt like an arrow as it swooped through the water. He was banging the net on the side of the pool when a pair of bare feet came towards him.

'You there,' she said casually. She wanted to know when the pool would be ready.

Jake paused a moment and met her eyes. They were blue-green like his and her hair was the same honey blond, only it was silky and long. They were almost the same height and had a similar lanky build. They might have been brother and sister.

Jake told her it would take at least one more day. And still she looked amused.

'Daddy has a machine that can do it quicker. It's automatic. A self-driven vacuum cleaner. It's got a mind of its own.'

She laughed and stuck a toe in the water.

'Just clear the stuff from the top. The machine can do the rest.'

She looked him over and then smiled and strolled back to the house.

Jake kept scooping up the leaves because he was afraid to stop. If he stopped he would have to work out what to do next. She didn't seem interested in his name or who he was. She didn't even acknowledge that he was someone new. The normal rituals didn't exist and it was as though he had always been there. He was a body with a function and would never be anything else.

Jake was ready to quit right there and let them find another pair of hands, another strong back. He didn't like the breezy way she ordered him around. But he had seen a flicker in her eyes as she had looked him over, and he stayed.

The next day she was doing laps when he arrived. The machine was purring across the tiles on the bottom. Back and forward it went as though it were powered by remote control. But Jake could see the electric cord that connected it to the mains in the house. He smiled to himself and imagined the possibilities. Aqua blue shot through with live, crackling veins of gold.

When she saw him standing by the pool she flipped over and began to backstroke, her shoulders arched back, thrusting her torso out of the water. She steamed through the water then tumbled just at the right moment to kick off from the opposite end. On the return lap, the machine passed beneath her dragging its cord across her path. One moment she was Cleopatra cruising down the Nile, then her arm caught the loop and she spluttered, her rhythm and composure lost, before disentangling herself and swimming on.

She heaved herself on to the side of the pool and waved him over. She raised a hand for him to help her up and stood beside him dripping on to the tessellated paving, still holding his hand. As her breathing slowed she let his hand drop and twitched a smile.

All that morning he saw her wandering around the garden as though she didn't know what to do with herself. Preparations were being made for some kind of celebration. Jake had seen the caretaker stringing paper lanterns through the trees around the courtyard. A truck had come and unloaded crates of champagne. There were caterers fixing a spit. Some men dressed in black were setting up a sound system in the pergola.

Later that afternoon Jake was in the shed trying to get the lawn-mower started. It was dark and he was fumbling with the petrol can. He heard the door open and when he turned around she was standing right behind him, luminous in a white sundress. She shifted restlessly on the spot, her leather sandals squeaking. He asked her what all the fuss was about and she said it was for her eighteenth birthday. The party was that evening but she was sick of waiting. She wanted it to happen right now.

'I've always been impatient.'

She reached forward, took the petrol can from him and placed it on the bench.

Afterwards Jake remained in the shed staring at the footprints in the dust where she had stood. He had lifted her skirt to find her naked underneath. Her skin and hair smelled of coconut oil. Rich and edible. His fingers slipped easily between her legs. She made a low sound and rubbed against him. She swayed from side to side, then forward and back, as she pressed her head into the curve of his shoulder. She moved with total concentration. He barely had to move his hand. She knew exactly what she wanted and how to get it.

For a while he was mesmerised by her rocking body. He pressed himself against her and could feel her grip tightening as her fingers dug into his skin. Her breath was rapid and she was moving faster. So far she had made no moves of her own. Her hands remained clasped to his shoulders. Jake murmured something in her ear but she didn't respond. She thrust herself against his fingers but no longer seemed conscious of him. Hesitantly, he lifted one of her hands from his shoulder and was guiding it down his jeans, when suddenly she was rigid and gasping. She sighed deeply, her body relaxing, and slowly drew away.

Jake let his arms drop. This had never happened to him before. A girl just taking what she wanted without a word. Usually it was him who took the lead. Usually there was no time for all that in the furious rush to get it over and done.

He watched as she smoothed down her dress. It was a signal that the encounter was over and he made no effort to stop her. She walked out on unsteady feet into the bright light of the garden.

FOUR

RUBEN IS STILL HALF asleep. He moves slowly about the cafe and whenever a car passes, his eyes track its path. Most dreams, he thinks, would seem comic afterwards if the sadness didn't cling. Like Marie taking off with a nineteen-year-old student in a battered VW after cleaning out his stock of chocolate bars. She looked ten years younger and happier than he had seen her in years. As they drove away Ruben noticed his best billiard cue sticking out the window like a surfboard. The cafe had become a dark cave with oil dripping from the ceiling and the sound of the deep-fry sizzling somewhere in its depths.

The hiss of steam from the cappuccino machine deepens to a muffled roar as the milk froths up to the top of the stainless steel jug. Still lost in the remnants of his dream, Ruben does not hear the door open. It's not until the girl is at the counter that he notices her. Loose strands of hair are plastered around her face. The rest is back in a ponytail. Her cheeks are flushed from running. Her dark eyes check him out. Then she looks around, searching for somebody.

'Is Marie here?'

'Not up yet. Can I help?'

Ruben holds back the froth with a long spoon and lets the milk almost fill the cup. He tops it up with a thick head and shakes chocolate powder over the dissolving bubbles. The girl watches him closely.

'You'll have to show me how it's done,' she says.

Ruben stares at her and then nods.

'Hannah?'

'That's me.'

'You need a shower.'

Hannah tugs at her running shorts and wipes her forehead. She wonders if he can smell the sweat. Marie had said that Ruben didn't waste his words.

'Guess I do.'

At lunchtime a bus pulls up and suddenly the cafe is full. Hannah is staring into a crowd of sunburnt faces demanding hamburgers, chips, roast beef and dim sims. She concentrates on serving each person in turn, afraid of overlooking someone who has been waiting longer than the rest. Ruben works at the grill behind her and never turns to face the customers. He consults the slips of paper she places on his right and calls out the numbers when the order is filled. He says it's the only way he can survive the summer. She can't help feeling she's been left to the wolves.

A man who has taken one bite from his steak sandwich thrusts it in her face. 'This is raw,' he growls. As she tosses the flesh back on the grill, Ruben leans toward her and speaks in a low voice. Hannah looks up at him, surprised. Her lips twitch as she stifles a laugh. He has eyes in the back of his head. Taking a deep breath, Hannah composes herself and faces the customer again.

The cowbell on the door rattles. More people, fresh from the beach, are shuffling across the tiled floor, creating trails of sand. Hannah reaches into the hot food servery where the light is intense. She is counting baked potatoes into a brown paper bag when she glances through the slanting glass. A pair of eyes are watching her from the far corner of the cafe. The owner of the eyes is sitting at the bench by the window, not drinking or eating or even smoking. He doesn't smile when she meets his gaze but neither does he look away. She has the feeling he has been watching her for some time. The crowd shifts, blocking her view and when she looks again, he's disappeared.

When the lunchtime crowd has gone Ruben makes her a coffee and they sit at one of the tables. Hannah takes off her shoes and flexes her toes. Ruben watches the muscles in her calves as they tense and relax. He hadn't wanted any help for the summer but when Marie mentioned her student friend, he saw his chance. There was so much he needed to know. At first Marie had been content with the Open Learning programs on the radio. She would get up early to make a tape because the classes went to air at a ridiculous hour. Sometimes Ruben could hear her in the loungeroom arguing with the voices the way she did when she got angry with people on TV.

Ruben could see that it was a hard way to study and he wasn't surprised when she enrolled at the university in the city. After that, nothing could stop her. Marie told him little of what she did on her 'campus' days. He wasn't even sure that she had to go. Everything she needed seemed to come in the mail. She could have been making it up for all he knew but he was too proud to ask. It made him feel old. He was trapped in the past, she was moving on.

As if for conversation, Ruben asks about life as a student.

Hannah laughs. Her voice defiant. 'I've dropped out.' She pauses dramatically. 'So I could work here.'

She hugs her knees to her chest observing his shock.

'Only joking. I wasn't happy, that's all. I got sick of studying. After a while you stop taking things in. I had to get out of my head.'

'I thought it was one big party.'

Hannah shrugs. 'If it was, I missed it.'

The one club she'd tried joining was the boardriders club. It seemed the best way to learn. But she was the only girl, and they didn't take her seriously. They thought she was a groupie, like the girls that hung around surfers at the beach. She decided then that she would be better off living by the sea and learning to surf the proper way. She could see this lot weren't interested in teaching her. And anyway, they weren't real surfers. They were university boys.

Ruben starts to clear the table.

'Marie loves it.'

'Of course she does. She's not filling in time like the rest of us.'

The university was full of bored students straight from school. You could hear them shifting around in tutorials. All their lives had been spent in classrooms. They had wandering legs and nowhere to go. But Marie knew this was her only chance.

Hannah follows Ruben back behind the counter. She hands him the plates and cups so he can stack them in the machine. Ruben notices her brown hands against the white porcelain. He tries to keep his voice detached.

'Does she have many friends?'

'Why don't you ask her?' she says, remembering the first time they met when Marie was demonstrating for a first year prac. Hannah had bounded up to her after the class and said she recognised her from the cafe. Marie wasn't pleased at being 'found out' and for a long time refused to talk about her other life. Later, when she invited Hannah to work at the cafe, Hannah knew she'd finally won her friend's trust.

Ruben snaps the door of the dishwasher shut and turns the dial. He says nothing. But silence sounds like a confession, so he breaks it.

'What will you do then?'

'Something I've always wanted.' Hannah stops sucking on her lemonade and grins. 'I'm gonna surf.'

Ruben smiles and scratches his neck.

'They'll eat you alive,' he says.

'You can't scare me with sharks.'

'The surfers, Hannah.'

Hannah's first lessons in the cafe are never forgotten. She learns the importance of cold, fresh milk to make a frothy cappuccino and how to wield an electric knife without losing a finger. She learns the secrets of enduring the lunchtime rush and how to make a spider that doesn't curdle. She learns how to make a sandwich without her hands ever touching the bread. She learns other things too from the locals who, surprised by the new face behind the counter, tell her stories about the town and its people that years of holiday-making might never have disclosed.

Hannah listens as she wipes down the tables or stacks the fridge with fruit juice and milk. There are two shifts of regulars, as predictable as the tides. Both come from the sea. In the morning the last of the town's fishermen wander in and pluck knitted beanies from balding heads. They come smelling fishy. Having cleaned and gutted the morning's catch and fed the entrails to the pelicans at the pier, they breakfast on fried bacon, eggs and sausages. They drink their coffee from soup mugs and talk quietly about the dying trade on this side of the bay.

In the evening the surfers lean their boards against the brick wall by the carpark and lounge under the umbrellas. They sit on the wooden tables with their legs wide apart or stand with one foot resting on a bench. They pass around fat roll-your-owns that send wafts of dope into the cafe. Their legs are wiry and brown up to mid-thigh where their boardshorts begin. Sometimes they show each other the small ulcers they've got from the salty water. They make jokes about chaffing or growths in their ears from the cold. On land they look twitchy, restless. In the water they're transformed. On her morning runs Hannah has seen them in their rubber suits. They move from land to sea like seals lumbering off the rocks and into their element.

Hannah watches their cars pull in across the gravel outside the cafe and her stomach turns over. At first they do not speak to her as the fishermen do. Only when they leave the group and come inside for a packet of cigarettes or box of matches, do they linger at the counter and ask her questions. When she takes their orders, she hears them talking about Spooks, Snatches, Gumboots, Quarantine

Station and Riding School No. 69. They might as well be speaking in code.

One hot evening, after a week at the cafe, she comes out carrying three milkshakes without a tray. Her sweat-soaked dress is clinging to her back. She almost trips on the bottom step but regains her balance before the milk is spilt. 'Whoa,' someone cries. They come forward to take the drinks and the mood is easy. Seagulls hover at a distance then edge closer, waiting for scraps. Hannah stands with her hands dangling at her sides, wanting to join in. She searches for the face with those watchful eyes, but she can't see him there. She would like to ask them who he is, but doesn't know how to begin.

'Look,' she says, lifting her arm as though to toss the seagulls something. The birds squawk and rise in unison, anticipating food. They float for a moment before sinking back to earth.

'Dumb birds,' says Mitch, the dark-haired one.

'Scavengers,' says someone else.

Hannah steers the talk back to surfing. She wants their advice.

'So where's this Gumboots and Snatches?' she asks, head cocked slightly to one side.

There are snorts of laughter. Hannah's face goes hot. Tim, who is the boldest of them, jumps off the table and comes up close. His smile is sardonic. He is performing for the boys and she knows she is about to suffer.

'Snatches,' he announces, one hand at the height of her belly and the other at the top of her thighs, 'is between here, and here.'

They roar and whistle. Hannah looks around at them. Some stare at the ground. Others laugh openly into her eyes. If only she could say something smart. Turn the joke back on them, or act like she doesn't care. But she can't even raise a smile.

She takes a sharp breath as though to speak, then turns about and goes inside.

FIVE

THE ROOM STINKS OF alcohol in its purest form. Marcus squats on the floor surrounded by newspapers on which he has placed his latest finds. Afternoon sun through the venetian blinds falls in yellow bars across the assorted objects. There is a red sea-urchin and slate-pencil urchin which he has just boiled. After removing what he can of the fleshy remains with tweezers, he drops the spiky balls into a preserving jar of clear spirits and clips on the lid. Taking a turban shell from a bowl of warm, fresh water he uses an oyster knife to scrape at the encrustations. With a gull's feather dipped in hydrochloric acid he lightly brushes away algae stains and washes the shell with soap. He rubs it with mineral oil until the swirls of green and bandages of white give off a liquid sheen. Pleased with the effect, Marcus places his latest specimen in one of the glass cabinets where his collection is displayed.

The sea squirt he had gathered the week before is shrivelled and dried. He fingers its brittle, leathery case. Already it crumbles at his touch. He takes it firmly and closes his hand, crushing until powder falls between his fingers.

At first he kept everything, as new collectors tend to do. But he has forced himself to be ruthless and discard what can't be preserved rather than watch it decay. When Ellen was dying of cancer, Marcus found that all emotion shut down. Nothing seemed to touch him. In the hospital bed her head looked strangely enlarged against her shrunken body beneath the sheet. It was beyond comprehension how all that flesh could disappear, leaving nothing but hollows and protruding bones. Then the day came when they pulled the sheet up over her face.

A black wave that dredges up the sunless depths, a wave that arcs so high it drags down the sun, stars and moon from the sky and turns the day to pitch.

For a year after her death he was stunned and lived like a robot. The only thing that kept him going was Jake. He knew that Jake could not be allowed to witness the wreckage of his mind. In the evenings he would make his son's dinner but forget to eat himself. A glass of ale was all he seemed to need. Hanging from the back of the truck in the early mornings, he would slip into a daze as he stared at the mound of freshly rotting rubbish until a shout or a whistle from one of the men brought him back.

On the anniversary of her death he was looking in the mirror and it struck him the way his collarbone protruded at the top of his shirt. There were ripples in his sternum. His face was gaunt, his blue eyes looked back at him from dark hollows. His clothes were all too big. He saw that he was doing to himself what the cancer had done to Ellen.

Marcus picks up a giant cuttlefish and wonders why he bothered with it. He already has enough of the stuff to satisfy a cage full of budgies. Next to it is another member of the class Cephalopoda, a ram's horn, its delicate spiral in perfect condition. It's the first one he has found undamaged. Of this class, the jewel for Marcus is the paper nautilus—the *argonauta*—in whose protective chambers the female of the species lays her eggs.

He saw one in a glass case at the local historical society and was amazed that it could survive the pounding surf. Its corrugated body curled like a foetus and looked tissue fine. The attendant told him how they were washed ashore after storms like ships blown off course. None had been found on the peninsula for many years.

That day in the museum the idea of the paper nautilus had lodged in his brain and spawned. He had become a collector over time, one find leading to another until he was praying for storms instead of waiting to see what the ocean tossed up. At night he found himself dreaming about wavy volutes and cowry shells, dog whelks and New Holland spindles.

A whole universe inside it. Shells, jellyfish, driftwood and deckchairs, bladder-wrack, corrugated iron, car tyres and starfish spiral down the deserted main street.

When the council started dredging for sand to salvage the Front Beach, Marcus was there every day before dawn sifting through the dumped, off-shore grains, a miner panning for gold. Out toward the shipping channel he could see the spout of the dredger spewing water back in to the bay as it sucked in the sand. There were mud oyster shells in abundance but they were as common as pebbles and only good for skipping on the water. No longer silky under foot, the sand was thick with broken pipis, the frilly bits of scallops and crushed cockles. What the sea had claimed, man claimed back. From the whole, reconstructed beach, the only real finds were a complete pheasant shell and a ribbed cowry.

Marcus thought about taking up diving but decided against it. Conchologists claimed that live shells made the best specimens. In lustre, color and sculpture they were said to be superior to those whose host had long since died. But for Marcus it was too much like piracy, like plundering the sea, to disturb their habitat and prise the living creatures from behind their little white doors. Although he liked to fossick in rock pools at low tide, he tried—not always successfully—to resist the easy looting of these miniature worlds. Sometimes the image of his groping hand, magnified by the water, and the sight of all life fleeing at his intrusion, was enough to stop him. What he liked best was to walk along the beach and stumble upon the unexpected. A pearly glint or half submerged cone in the sand.

In the loungeroom behind the shop Hannah rubs oil into Marie's shoulders and back. The oil lights up her lean body and deepens its curves. Marie lies on her belly with the straps of her bathers pulled to her waist, just as she lay all day on the sand.

On an empty stretch of the Long Beach far from the crowds between the flags, she had lost herself in *Wuthering Heights*. It was the most luxurious thing she'd done in ages. An on-shore breeze took the edge off the sun until late afternoon. Then the wind died away and the temperature dropped. Although the air was cool her skin gave off a feverish heat. When she went to stand up she almost fainted. By the time she got home her head was dazed and her shoulders were tight and raw.

Ruben shrugged when she pulled back her shirt and showed him. She wanted too much too soon, he said. Marie examined the cracked skin and the tender pink tissue beneath it. She didn't mind the pain. Stinging and soreness were summer sensations, like the smell of Coppertone. It meant that her body was waking after a long winter.

Sitting to one side, Hannah draws her hands down Marie's back to the vestige of the human tail. She circles it slowly with her fingers until Marie moans with pleasure.

'The coccyx,' Marie says savouring the word. 'I'd wag it if I could.'

'When I stroke my cat right there she gets this look in her eye and her tongue starts to flicker,' Hannah says.

They laugh and Marie's shoulders heave off the floor. She is surprised at how much she enjoys being in Hannah's hands. Sometimes the age difference brings out a strange tenderness in them both.

Hannah leans toward her, rubbing the residue down Marie's arms. She can feel the energy locked in her muscles as though her fingers were curled in a fist.

'Ruben's right of course. I stayed out too long. But I couldn't help it. I'd forgotten how good it felt. Like thawing out. I've spent too much bloody time climbing in and out of that cool room. It's got into my bones.'

Hannah massages her friend's neck, blows on the patches of red and tells her to relax. She places her thumbs either side of the nob at the top of the spine and forces them upward. Marie has one of those bodies that radiates tension and needs coaxing into pleasure. Even Hannah can see that Ruben isn't the coaxing type. He would like to be, she imagines, but he probably doesn't know how to start.

'Maybe Ruben would give you a massage, if you asked him,' Hannah says.

Marie laughs harshly. 'Not any more.' She lowers her head to her folded arms and closes her eyes. 'I used to like watching him with his motorbike, oiling the parts.' Her voice is full of amazement, as if the thought of it baffles her now. His fingers knew exactly what to do and where all the bits went. She liked his confidence and sureness. His self-possession.

'Ruben rode a motorbike?'

'Not for long. He stuck it in the back shed, along with everything else.'

Marie twitches as Hannah's hands travel down her back. She instructs Hannah to expose her cheeks.

Hannah wonders if Marie has sunstroke. She isn't normally like this. She doesn't like revealing clothes and she keeps her body to herself.

Hesitantly, Hannah drags the bathers down expecting pearly white. She is shocked to see they're burnt.

'Looks like you've been roasted,' Hannah says, pouring on more oil that seeps between the crack.

'Feels like I'm on heat. Like those baboons that parade their swollen red buttocks.'

Marie had been at the zoo the week before with her six-year-old nephew when they saw it happen. Robby became excited and asked what it meant. Marie didn't know what to say. She'd never wanted children of her own. It wasn't her job to explain the facts of life. His mother or father could do that. Marie told him the baboon was showing off, but Robby wanted to know why.

'So what did you tell him?'

'I said she wanted a fuck.'

'You didn't.'

'No. I said she was hungry. Which is kind of true. So Robby threw in one of his Cheezles. Then whamo, I got this idea for my thesis. The eating habits of primates in captivity.'

'Brilliant.'

'I thought so.'

They laugh again, a delirious, light-headed laughter that leaves them feeling exhausted.

Jake is heading for the laundry to get a mop for Ruben when he hears them. For a moment he can't work out what's going on. Marie is lying almost naked on the loungeroom carpet and that girl is crouched over her, massaging her arse. He hovers in the doorway, reminded of a painting he once saw. A black woman washing her mistress in a bathhouse full of green light. His father had dragged him along to a gallery and he was bored. He had moved quickly from painting to painting, registering nothing until the sight of these women made him pause. He'd felt he was invading something private, something he shouldn't be witnessing. It was like peering through a keyhole but he couldn't draw himself away. He stood in front of it until his father came in search of him.

Hannah looks up and he is caught, once again, watching. Framed by the doorway he appears taller than she had thought. She recognises him immediately. Those eyes scrutinising her. She notices the way his body shifts, his muscular shoulders, his matted hair, his eyes bluer than the sea he spends his days immersed in. Hannah knows a surfer when she sees one. He is standing with his arms crossed, unsure what to do. Before he can disappear, Hannah gets off her knees and solemnly offers him her hand.

Jake is slow to respond. Her formality takes him by surprise. He can't work out if she's serious or not.

Marie lies between them. She pulls up her bathers and rolls on to her back. She looks from one to the other.

'Stay for dinner Jake. You need a haircut.'

The billiard table sits like a cultivated lawn in the middle of the room. A shaded bulb hangs low over the expanse of green. Ruben circles it slowly, pausing now and then to take his eye to the level of the white and red balls. He lines up his cue and runs it back and forward over his thumb stopping just short of the ball. He straightens up and reaches for the chalk that hangs at one end of the table. Back in position, he is about to play a shot when Marie moves from a dark corner and into his sights. Impatiently he waves a hand at her and returns his attention to the ball. After a long pause she shifts to the right, just outside his field of vision.

The billiard table is another reason Ruben is never seen outside the cafe. He has turned his garage into a refuge. Behind its grey fibro walls he spends all his free hours refining his shots and working out strategies to hold his position as the town's top player. It's the simplicity of the game that appeals to him. Three balls, a cue and a table. He can study a shot from any angle and predict the way the balls will rebound. He can set up future shots in an endless chain reaction. Sometimes the look of it pleases him most of all. He thinks of the models scientists use to show the motion of molecules, or of sub-atomic particles, the protons and electrons that hurtle madly around the nucleus. One night, when the red ball was struck by the white, instead of the usual sharp clink, there was a dull crack. The red ball split in half and the two hemispheres went off in opposite directions, like spinning tops, as Ruben watched in wonder. For the first time he saw what was inside.

Marie takes her turn at the table. She pots the red ball with studied indifference. She plays again and misses an easy cannon. The balls slam into the cushion and ricochet across the baize. Ruben sighs and turns to Jake and Hannah.

'She won't try any more. I'm too far ahead.'

'Rubbish.'

Marie rams her cue back in the stand.

'Hannah, you play. I'll fix Jake.'

Hannah reaches for the scissors that Marie has placed on the shelf at the back wall. She snips the air.

'I'll do it.'

She looks at Jake. For the first time, he smiles at her. His teeth flash white against his tanned face. He leans back against the wall as though challenging her. Hannah takes him in. He has a gold sleeper in one ear and is wearing a ribbed mariner's jumper that's been through the tumble drier one too many times. It now barely reaches his waist.

She tries not to stare but there's a worn patch in his jeans either side of the zip.

Jake closes his eyes. The cold steel inches across his forehead. Shards of blond hair fall on his nose and cheeks and down to his shoulders. When Marie cut his hair she sat back calmly and surveyed her canvas. She has been cutting it for years. Before that, Marcus did it, and before that, his mother, but those memories are hazy. Hannah works from close range as though measuring each strand. As she leans toward him he can feel her breath on his face in warm, irregular puffs.

Hannah's hand shakes as she guides the blades down the side of his cheek. Jake has asked her to cut it all off—the shoulder length waves, everything. He wants it spiky and short. Punk-style. He hardly knows her and he has placed himself in her hands. She is flattered by the invitation but she cannot possibly do what he asks. She likes him the way he is. Something about him makes her think of the Elizabethans. A wild version. Like Christopher Marlowe must have been. She had once written an essay about Marlowe and his reckless ways. She can't imagine why Jake would want to change.

'Do what you like then,' he says.

Hannah can't tell if he's disappointed or not. Perhaps she has failed some test. Perhaps she's being uncool. She cautiously trims his fringe and the split ends. Then, without a word, she snips at the fine hairs above his lip which suggest a moustache and a faint snarl. His eyelids look like pale, quivering oysters just waiting to be sucked from their shells. They are the only part of his face untouched by the sun. The rest of his body is still but there's nothing calm about him. His cheek muscles clench; he is concentrating hard.

Behind them, Marie and Ruben are sniping at one another. Hannah wishes that they would take their argument somewhere else and leave Jake and her alone.

'Done,' she says, dropping her arms. She puts the scissors back on the shelf. There's the clink of billiard balls and the sound of feet across the lino.

Jake looks in the mirror and sees her standing behind him. In the dim light her pupils are wide and dark. She's waiting for his response. He studies his reflection, turning one way and then the other. She has done almost nothing and yet he likes what he sees.

'Jakey boy,' Ruben calls out from across the room. 'Has she told you she wants to surf?'

Jake raises his eyebrows and looks at her just like the bus driver did when he saw her board.

'Oh yeah?'

'I thought you might show her how.'

Jake runs a hand over his freshly cut hair and turns to Hannah.

'Sure. If that's what you want.'

It's over a week before Hannah hears from Jake and she's starting to think he has gone cold on the idea. Then he appears at the cafe one afternoon and says 'What about tomorrow?'

They go to Buddha, far from the prying eyes of the Long Beach. Hannah wonders why Jake is taking her.

They drive in silence. From the old highway they turn into a dirt track and bump along until the bush closes in and there's nowhere to go. Jake pulls out Hannah's board from the back of the Holden and hands it to her. It's wider than most and hard to get her arm around. The wax has melted and her hand slips along the rails. Jake slings the wetsuits over his shoulder as they make their way through the stunted banksia to the sand hills beyond.

The dunes are not a prelude to the beach but a country in themselves. On days like this, people hug the shade of buildings and trees rather than step into the searing light. But here there is no cover. Hannah thinks of deserts, how only nomads inhabit them. She's heard it said that they count the time in nights not days, and in this heat she can understand why. She measures the distance by the weight of her load. Her feet sink into the sand that flows like water down the slopes of each hill. There's something familiar about this terrain, the way it dissolves beneath her.

They cross a flat stretch of ground dotted with dead roots and petrified tree stumps. On top of a rise the wind blows sand in the air like the spray from a wave. Spinifex and small succulents are all that hold this shifting surface. On winter mornings, Jake tells her, the dunes are crusty with the cold. He runs across them in his bare feet knowing that as soon as he hits the water, his head will flash with white-hot pain like it did when he ate icecream as a kid.

They come out of the valley and suddenly the sea. Deepest blue against the powdery sky. A warm breeze at their backs. Jake points to the waves and with his finger traces their path as they break. Turning away from her, he strips and eases on his wetsuit like a second skin. His litheness shames her. She feels like a walrus in her shiny black pelt.

Jake picks up his board and is about to head off when Hannah touches his shoulder.

'Can you give me some hints.'

'Hints?'

'On how it's done. Like if I want to do a cutback followed by a re-entry on a left-hander, which foot should I have forward?'

Jake smiles slowly.

'The day you do a re-entry I'll be fucked. What have you been reading? Surfing in five easy steps? If you want to get real about surfing throw your books away.'

Jake drops his board.

There's not much to say, she thinks. Just get out there and do it. Paddling out the back'll be simple enough. Take the rip, and go with it. Like catching a bus.

'Don't take the rip,' Jake says, as though reading her thoughts. He's watching the parallel lines forming along the horizon. 'Stay in the shorebreak. It's looking a bit mean out there.'

There are many things Hannah wants to ask but already he's bolting across the sand. It's something she has noticed before. The way surfers always run down the beach. Never walk. As though it were an emergency and they had to get out there fast.

At the water's edge Hannah attaches the leg rope to her ankle and wades in. She paddles in Jake's direction but he's already gone. Lost in the waves.

The first one hits her like a shock. Her arms are working but she seems to be going backwards. She strokes hard, getting nowhere. Whitewater buffets her from all sides and it takes all her energy to remain flat on the board.

Eventually she reaches a spot where the water is less turbulent but murky. She feels the tug of a current running counter to the waves. Her movements are clumsy but to her surprise she is travelling outward. Peaks well up, but none of them break, keeping her path open.

When Hannah turns back, the shore looks distant. Waves that seemed like hillocks from the beach take on new dimensions as they rear above her. Her arms are beginning to ache. It would be so much easier to ditch her board and swim. When it was only her body and the sea, she was free to dive and weave. But manoeuvring the board is a major feat, like a tanker changing direction.

Jake is not much further out and as soon as he spots her, he shakes his head. Behind him a new set of waves is approaching and Hannah can see that they are much bigger than before. Every six or seven sets, she remembers, comes the freak one. Hannah feels the suction of the on-coming waves as she is pulled outward. Jake is jabbing the air urgently with a finger. He glances over his shoulder and positions himself for the first wave. Then he's swooping down the glittering face and cutting back into its fleshy shoulder. From behind him, she sees his head bobbing above the hump of white as he rides it all the way in.

Hannah begins to paddle toward the shore but finds that she's placing herself in the direct line of the on-coming waves. Everything is moving relentlessly to a point of impact. The water swells and lifts. As the wave unfurls with the force of the wide ocean behind it, she notices that an open corridor remains where the rip travels. She scrambles towards it, paddling hard. It looks like she will slip over the top of the first peak before it begins to crumble. But the wind is too light to hold up the wave and it rears unexpectedly, catching the tail of her board just as she glimpses what lies beyond.

The free fall backwards is just the beginning. All is white, roaring confusion. For what seems like hours she is flung about. Hungry for air she pushes toward the surface only to find that there is no surface. She is burying herself deeper. She swirls around looking for the light, the pressure in her chest growing. What made her think she could handle this? She kicks furiously, then tries to scissor her way up. Her arms claw at the water that presses in from all sides. She longs for the wide openness of the sky.

Something out of control, something frenzied is starting to whip around inside her. As she doubles up she catches sight of her thrashing arms and legs, and the shock of it makes her stop. She feels a tugging at her ankle. She remembers her leg rope. She grabs it and scrambles upward. As she pushes towards the surface, she has a terrible desire to open her mouth. She tells herself not to but just before she reaches the light, her lips part and the water pours in.

She bursts through, her body convulsing. Her board bobs near by, unconcerned, like a seagull on the skin of the ocean. She drapes herself across it, her shoulders heaving, her eyes closed. She breathes the sweetness of the air. The set of waves has passed above her and she drifts in its wake. The sea looks spent. All Hannah wants to do is lie on the coarse-grained beach and stare at the sky.

Jake sees her lying face down on the sand as he comes from the sea, the undertow dragging at his ankles. Water pours from his wetsuit in a warm flood. The firm sand jars beneath his step after hours of weightlessness. He wonders if she is asleep. She has draped her wetsuit out on the board and the leg rope is tied neatly around the tail. Her face is hidden beneath her hair.

He stands above her and casts a shadow. He would like to touch her back streaked white with salt. Her ochre body looks strong. She has athlete's legs and a compact shape. Not slender or fine-boned like the girls he has known from the mansions. They are beautiful in a glossy way that leaves him stunned. Where Hannah fits in Jake isn't sure, except that she comes from another place and that for all her education there are a lot of things she doesn't know much about. What puzzles him most is the way she seems to have no plans and yet talks of the future as though it were in her power.

'So, how was it?'

An eye peers at him from between ropes of hair.

'I nearly drowned,' she says, her voice muffled.

Jake shrugs. 'Everyone says that the first time. You get used to it.'

'To drowning?'

'Being wiped-out. It's unavoidable. You'll always come up.'

Hannah laughs bleakly. She sits up on her towel, her legs crossed. With her right hand she digs into the sand feeling the warmth give way to moist coolness. She doesn't think she can face going through that again. She has never been wiped-out before, not in any way.

'You make it look so easy. But it isn't. It's the hardest thing I've ever tried. Harder than physics.'

Almost nostalgically she adds, 'Do you know what made me want to do it? I read this poem when I was about ten years old. It was called 'The Surfer'. I always loved going down the beach but I hadn't taken much notice of surfers. They were just boys on boards. Then I read this poem. There was something about them after that.'

She begins to recite then stops to explain.

'I guess it's about a showdown. Between the surfer and the sea. But only the sea can win.'

She turns to him, her eyes shining.

Jake is packing up. There is something in her voice that makes him uneasy, impatient. She's got these dreamy ideas. *A showdown that only the sea can win.* What would a poet know?

'What d'you reckon now?' he asks.

Hannah brushes the sand from her hands and jumps up. She shakes her towel so hard it makes a loud crack. The sand blows back in her face. She is too ashamed to say.

'I'll keep trying.'

'It might take years, Hannah. Every day. All through the winter. That swell is straight from the Antarctic. Don't expect it to be easy.'

'Thanks for the encouragement.'

'D'you want me to bullshit?'

'Just a little.'

As they make their way back across the sand dunes, Jake hears her behind him, whispering the words of the poem to herself as if she were trying to cast a spell.

That night when Hannah closes her eyes, her body rises and falls with the waves. The day swims in her mind. The best times were the lulls between sets when she could sit astride the board and look around at the different colors of the ocean, the coastline stretching all the way to Cape Schanck where the white pillar of the lighthouse warned of the danger below; the lulls between those mountains of water that rose out of nowhere and were inescapable. She had spent more time dodging waves than paddling for them, diving down to the bottom of the ocean to grab handfuls of sand as the bulldozing foam passed above her. Wave after wave she came smack up against a wall of fear.

SIX

ANOTHER TUESDAY. MARIE UP early and gone before breakfast. Ruben watching her go from the carpark as he unstacks the benches from the tables outside the cafe. He wrestles the wooden shaft of the sun umbrella through the hole in the table and into the concrete block below. He attaches a bag of sand for extra ballast. Someone from the council would be coming around to check that he was securing the umbrellas properly. They didn't want a repeat of last summer when a gust of wind sent one flying along the Back Beach and speared a woman through the heart. Ruben remembers seeing the wreaths layed out on the sand after the funeral and how they floated out with the tide so that the sea was awash with petals. With an involuntary jerk, his hand goes up to his chest.

The term has ended but nothing has changed in the way that he hoped it would. Marie still thrashes the Falcon all the way to the city and stays until late in the evening. He can imagine her on the freeway sitting on the tail of the car in front until it moves to the other lane. She is always in a hurry, a hurry to get away. She says she is doing research at the State Library, and lately she has started talking about the zoo. It sounds crazy to him. She has the chance to lie in the sun and instead she heads for the city to bury herself in books. And always when she gets back, the petrol tank is full as though she's hiding something from him.

Sometimes he suspects she is being deliberately evasive just to taunt him. Ruben cannot bring himself to ask her straight out. He makes cryptic allusions and plans strategies as elaborate as those he applies in billiards—a game as much about deflection as it is about collision. He has questioned Hannah but that hasn't got him very far. She insists that the story about the zoo is true. And so far, he has no reason to doubt her.

On the radio Marie hears reports of bushfires breaking out around the countryside, and clouds of airborne ash and topsoil being driven south by the wind. Barely nine o'clock and already it's thirty degrees. As she parks the car outside the library she can feel the hot air thickening around her. On days like this her notepaper curls at the edges and the ink pours from her pen. She thinks of the cave she has made her own near London Bridge at the far end of the Long Beach. No matter how hot outside, it remains cool throughout the day. It's ten steps from the water and at high tide the waves surge into the entrance. On the cliff above is barbed wire marking the end of the beach and the beginning of the army camp. Danger signs with red crosses and black skulls warn trespassers of unexploded shells from training exercises. Apart from the surfers who pass by on their way to Spooks, no one else disturbs her there.

It would be easy, she supposes, to lie on the beach all day and not give another thought to bioclimatic zones, gorillas' foraging behavior or the dilemmas of anthropomorphism. Easy to forget the unexploded shells lying hidden in the scrub on the far side of the barbed wire. Easy not to step into the minefield of conflicting ideas and risk turning her life upside down. Easy, that is, if she could live with herself and with Ruben, and with her ever sharpening tongue. But it's not a question that she seriously entertains. It's cool enough under the high dome of the Reading Room, her cave of words with its concentric circles of desks and walls of books stacked all the way to the ceiling.

During the morning as she works Marie looks forward to lunch. A meal where someone waits on *her*, takes her order and brings her the food. There's a small place around the corner that regularly changes its menu. It's her one indulgence—a restaurant with table service. The one meal of the week she can eat without a trace of guilt or compulsion to thrust her fingers down her throat. She has got to know the waiters. She is relieved to find that most of them are actors—their real work is done elsewhere. She likes the way they recite the day's specials in beautifully projected voices.

Marie understands this double life—playing the part of a waitress who longs to be someone else. To anybody who meets her in the cafe, she is just the woman behind the counter who takes the money and serves the food. She hates the way strangers can be so familiar, presuming to know who she is because of where she works. And then there are the regulars who need to believe that nothing will change, that she will always be there, serving up 'the usual' without having to be asked.

Ruben isn't fooled by her performance. She suspects

that he has been questioning Hannah about what she does on campus. Marie never told him much, partly out of anger that he showed no interest, and partly because she didn't want to hurt him. He seemed to believe that when it came to her study, he had nothing to offer, nothing to say. It was a surprise the other day, when he picked up one of her textbooks that was lying on the couch and ventured, 'Must read this sometime. Discover what you're up to.' Marie thought he was having a go at her and was about to tell him to lay off when she realised he was serious. He was cradling the book in his palm and fingering the glossy pages as though he really believed it might hold the answers to their lives.

Instead of encouraging him, Marie found herself repelled by the effort he was making, and told him not to bother. He seemed to think he could simply pick up a book and discover what it had taken her years to comprehend. As if it were as simple as flinging open a door. Marie knew it was a hard and painful process; it meant confronting all sorts of cherished beliefs and letting them go. And once your eyes were opened, there could be no going back. But if there was one thing she had learned since returning to study, it was that there were two options in life as the body aged. The mind could harden and settle into its comfortable, unquestioned ways, or it could be forced through sheer will to remain open to the unexpected; to all that was new and strange and threatening.

Hannah is sitting on the back porch finishing her orange juice when Jake arrives. The air is crisp; the light still powdery as the day begins. Some mornings he finds her in the hammock slung between two verandah posts. One time she had drifted back to sleep, her right arm hanging loose so that her fingers brushed the wooden boards below. She looked like she was reclining in the back of a boat lazily testing the water. Like a girl beneath a parasol in some Edwardian painting where the light was always dappled and the mood timeless. It seemed to Jake that her life was like that. She did what she pleased always knowing she had something to go back to, no matter how far she ventured up the river and into the trees.

Hannah hears his car coming down the driveway. It noses past the side of the house. She can pick the sound of his engine anywhere, even in a busy street. She turns, knowing she will see his shock of blond hair above the wheel, his elbow resting in the open window, his voice crying out 'hey bird' in that ironic way. It makes her smile to think of it.

She grabs her gear and climbs in the passenger seat. Grains of sand graze her thighs as she slides across the vinyl. Jake reverses all the way to the corner of the street. The car makes a high-pitched whine like it is about to launch into space. He does a sharp u-turn at the highway and sees two girls crossing the road after their morning swim. Veering left he lets the wheels skid in the gravel. A shower of small stones flies in their direction as he accelerates away. The girls jump back and watch the car disappear. Hannah can read the dismay on their faces.

She stares at him. 'What was that for?'

'Dunno,' Jake says. 'Just felt like it.'

Unexpectedly, Hannah laughs. 'When I was at state school there was this boy I was mad on. He had red hair and freckles. I was too afraid to tell him how much I liked him so I got a stick and hit him over the head.'

Jake cracks a smile. 'Hit me,' he says, teasingly.

Without thinking, Hannah punches his shoulder and quickly looks away. She hadn't meant to touch him. She was going to feint like a boxer but then her fist connected, and hard.

Jake smothers a wince with a mocking smile.

'That's some left hook.'

'I didn't mean to. It just happened.'

'You're stronger than you think.'

Hannah wishes she could believe him. She turns to the window. The windsock above the pub on the hill is swollen and pointing toward the Strait. It is a good sign. The waves will be clean.

They drive through the silent township and past the closed blinds of Ruben's. There are no other cars on the road. Everything is fresh and still and shimmering as though the world were behind glass and if they drove fast enough, they could crash through. Just over the hill is the Back Beach. Hannah experiences a familiar sensation. Her bowels stirring. The blue opens out before them, neat furrows with white edges feathered by the wind.

'Take a look at that,' Jake says.

Two small headlands form a protected bay making it ideal for learners. The waves move more sluggishly here than at other breaks, slowed by the outer reef.

Jake helps Hannah with her board and waits until she

has her wetsuit on. Although he's easier with her now, he still acts as if she's some distant relative whom he has been asked to chaperone. He zips her up and cries 'Go for it,' as he springs back up the steps to the carpark.

Even at this time of the morning other beginners are there, floundering in the shorebreak and eating sand with the dumpers. The first rush of excitement subsides as Hannah watches the Holden wind its way back up the hill. Once she's alone she has to work hard to keep her spirits up and not dwell on what happened at Buddha. Jake admitted to her afterwards that he'd chosen badly. It was a tricky break that only the experienced could handle. Ever since, Hannah has had to force herself back in the water.

Each morning she wakes before the alarm goes off and does her exercises. Deep, controlled breathing for staying calm when a set looms; push-ups for paddling; burpees for that distant day when she gets to her feet; squats and sit-ups for manoeuvrability. She is used to this kind of routine. It was the way she got through school, except that then instead of exercises, she spent her mornings studying or practising the piano. At school she never let up. She was sure that if she did she'd fall flat on her face. Her teachers would discover she wasn't the achiever they thought her to be. There were students who cruised through their exams with top marks and a minimum of effort. They fascinated Hannah. They were the naturals, the ones who took success for granted.

In her final year cracks started to appear in her performance. She wasn't all that musical but her determination had always carried her in the past. By the time she realised she wasn't coping, it was too late to stop. She was committed; she had to go on. Part of the preparation for the final practical exam was a piano masterclass. Before puberty she knew no fear. She could sit with her legs dangling from the piano stool in front of a crowd of people and attack a Bach Prelude as if it had been written for her. But now as she sat in the hall listening to the other students flying through their Mozart Fantasias and Chopin Nocturnes, she knew that events had moved beyond her control. Her name was being called and she was walking across the wooden boards to the platform. In the polished veneer of the baby grand she could see her stricken face. She watched her fingers flitting across the keys as though they belonged to someone else. She held her breath, knowing it could not last. When her fingers stopped moving it was almost a relief. She stood up and announced that she couldn't continue. The master of the class looked at her coldly and lowered his voice.

'You should not be here.'

Hannah could only agree. She picked up her music and headed down the long aisle to the 'Exit' sign at the back of the hall.

Hannah watches the undertow suck back the shorebreak in deep, gasping breaths. A nice little wave is peeling off the inner reef but the idea of going out makes her stomach tighten. *You should not be here.* She thinks of the yellowing newspaper photograph on the kitchen door at the beach house. A shot of the Back Beach in a gnarly mood with curved arrows pointing to where the rips usually run. 'Danger. Don't Swim Here'. It was published ten years ago not long after a young boy had gone missing. There were rumours of a whirlpool that sucked unsuspecting swimmers down to a hidden shelf under which they would become trapped.

In Hannah's memory of summer holidays there are always children drowning or being stung by blue-ringed octopuses or mauled by sharks or bitten by venomous spiders. Yet the only suffering she witnessed was the suffering she inflicted on various small animals plucked from the rock pools, dried out in the sun and then buried in a flowerbed decorated with sticks and fading shells. Death was a game played-out in the garden and then left behind when the evening fell. With the darkness came the comforting smell of the barbecue; the incense of mosquito coils; the saying of grace with hands clasped around the table on the back verandah.

As for the danger of the rips, she knows better now. What is death to a swimmer is a short cut to a surfer, an escalator running through a peak hour crowd.

Jake reckons she dwells too much on what can go wrong. He says she has read too many poems about the sea, as if there's something morbid in it. And perhaps there is. She lingers over his surfing magazines with their high gloss photos of monstrous Hawaiian waves and tiny bodies in free fall, frozen mid-plummet just before close-out. She likes the sequence shots the best, the ones that trace the surfer's descent frame by frame, from the precarious take-off to the broken board washed up on the beach.

Hannah gets to her knees and finds a chunk of wax that smells of strawberries. She rubs it across the fibreglass surface until it forms a collection of scabs. She tests the grip with a sweep of her hand. Satisfied, she bundles her clothes up in her towel and marches towards the water. At the far end, the large rock pool is almost covered by the high tide. Behind the headland are sandstone cliffs that form a ragged shoreline until they fall away at the Long Beach where Jake has gone.

The afternoon seems to have no end. Hannah sits by the window looking out over the deserted streets. On stinking hot days the cafe is dead. The cowbell over the door hasn't rung since lunch. The whole town has gone to the beach. Hannah has wiped every surface, mopped the floor, cleaned the cappuccino machine and restocked the shelves. She has given up searching for things to do. A fat blowfly buzzes in the corner, growing more frantic each time it butts the window. Ripples of heat shimmer above the road that disappears in the direction of the Long Beach.

Hannah can almost hear the squeals of delight from the children plunging into the waves and the cheers of the crowds that hover at the water's edge. So many of them, just standing there. *Neither in far nor out deep.* Legs planted in the sand. Growing out of it. Bodies tangled like kelp at their feet.

She can see it all. The beach is kilometres long but everybody stays between the flags, trading off the sense of expansiveness they might have enjoyed for the safety of the group. Further up towards the Sphinx, away from the rest, the surfers gather. Or more precisely, their girlfriends, left lying on the sand, their bodies shifting under the naked sun.

Hannah knows the story. It's an old one and not about

to change overnight. Up north where the weather is warmer and the beach culture stronger, it's not so divided. But in these colder waters, she misses the company of women. She tried roping Marie in for a session but they knew it was doomed. Ruben was keen on the idea and even made them a picnic lunch. But after a half-hearted stint in the shorebreak, Marie dumped her board on the sand and retired to one of the rock pools where she could sit and read.

There's one other woman surfer Hannah has seen. The first time was at the Long Beach, late one afternoon, when she and Jake were sitting on their boards, stirring the water with their feet, spinning themselves around in circles.

Further up, two other surfers were also waiting in the dying swell for some sign of a wave. The light was fading but she could tell from their silhouettes that one was a woman. She looked so good Hannah knew she must be a local. Jake said she was one of the best around. She used to live in the town and hang out with the boys until she got a job in the city.

As they made their way up the cliff to the carpark, Hannah watched the woman ride a last wave into shore. Her style was different from other surfers she'd seen. She didn't attack the wave so much as flow with it, swooping across it with a poise and ease that Hannah could only envy.

SEVEN

HANNAH MAKES HER WAY home from the cafe along the old highway. At the sides of the road, the nasturtiums and pig-face glow like coral in the shallows. Colors flare as the evening falls. By the time she reaches the house it is dark and the stars are out. At the driveway she flicks open the letter box and digs in her hand to find a soft, pliable package. She recognises the writing and tears at the brown paper. It is something made of cloth. She shakes it out and holds it up. A white cotton dress with a delicate batik pattern and a halter neck. It is close-fitting with small slits up the sides of the skirt to allow for freer movement. There is no note with it, but for Hannah the dress speaks, and it says all she needs to know.

She lies the dress flat on her bed and fingers the soft cloth. She imagines Jake walking into the shop and standing awkwardly among the racks of women's clothes; the shop assistant holding out selections and Jake mentally dressing and undressing her in the various styles. She can see his eye fix on one particular dress. The shop assistant smiles and folds it between layers of tissue paper. Jake takes the parcel home but cannot face handing it to her, so he goes to a post box and drops it into the slot.

The next morning she's wearing it as she waits for him on the verandah. He's getting out of the car when he sees her. He stops midway and Hannah notices how his whole body seems to burn with a slow blush.

'Nice dress,' he drawls.

Hannah stands in front of him. She spins around and sticks her arms out at right angles like a scarecrow. She drops them and steps toward him.

'Just right.'

'Yeah,' he says. 'Perfect.'

'But it's too good to wear to the beach.'

'Wear it tonight,' Jake says casually. 'The boys are going to the pictures.'

Hannah struggles to keep a serious face. A smile twitches at the corners of her mouth.

'Is that an invitation?'

'Of course.'

'What about the boys?'

'What *about* the boys?'

Hannah stares at the ground. She is thinking of those laughing eyes outside the cafe when she asked them about Snatches. She doesn't know how to explain.

'Nothing. I'll be there.'

It's one of those summer nights when the heat doesn't fade with the light. Not even a sea breeze. Like being in a room with no windows or doors. Hannah walks from the cafe up the main street, her bare feet warmed by the bitumen and her body wrapped in the batik dress. In spite of the heat she feels light and airy. She smoothes the fabric down her thighs and glances at her reflection in the shopfronts. The way it fits so well makes her shiver.

The town is lit up and outside the picture theatre a

queue is forming. It might be the streetlights or the mauve sky, but everyone's skin has a liquid sheen as though they were all underwater. There are family groups and young people in t-shirts and jeans coolly eyeing everyone who passes. She hears someone say *the girl from the cafe* and tries to melt into the crowd.

Hannah steps into the deep red foyer where the temperature is even higher than outside. When she was sixteen, she went alone to see a movie at one of the big city cinemas. She liked the anonymity of the dark theatre. Not long after she had chosen her seat, a boy began moving stealthily down the rows towards hers. Leaving a trail of soft thuds behind him he edged from seat to seat as though drawn to her by some sixth sense. By the time the feature had begun, he was at her side and it was impossible to concentrate. She looked sidelong at him and caught his profile lit up by the flickering light. To her surprise he wasn't a creep. His face was soft and round like an angel's. With his eyes fixed straight ahead, he reached out and took her hand and gave it a gentle, reassuring squeeze. His skin was moist but not sweaty, and she let him stroke her palm as she watched the figures moving about on the screen. They had no substance, they were simply tricks of light. She intertwined her fingers with his and waited for what would happen next.

Soon he untangled his fingers and shifted them lightly to her thigh. Hannah shivered and shot him a cautious glance. The boy smiled back at her and sank deeper into his seat, letting his hand rest where it lay. Hannah felt herself go flickery all over, like she had slipped into the film itself. She was about to place her hand on his jeans, when it flashed through her mind where all this could lead.

The next thing she knew she was jumping up and stumbling across people's knees as she made her way to the aisle. She headed for the nearest exit and into the stark light of the street. Rubbish was overflowing from a bin near the entrance, and everyone who went by looked washed-out and tired. All the mystery had gone. Immediately she wished she was back inside.

Hannah examines her watch. People are moving inside and Jake and the others are nowhere in sight. There are faces she recognises and she nods as they brush past her. Over the tops of the heads she searches for some sign of his.

The bell is ringing when she sees Jake's car parked on the other side of the main street, the pink gingham curtains drawn in the back. She waits for him to get out but nothing happens. As she starts to cross the road, she hears laughter coming from inside the car and what sounds like a girl's voice. The Holden begins to rock and a male voice hoots the way they do when someone catches a good wave. For a horrible moment Hannah wonders if the whole thing has been staged for her benefit. Some kind of joke or Jake's way of playing it cool. Or perhaps it was the boys' idea.

She stands on the median strip unable to go forward or back. She had thought things would be different now. She had thought she would know where she stood. But she is getting a sinking feeling that it might always be like this.

A sea breeze has finally sprung up and is whipping at her dress. Hannah glances over her shoulder. Everyone has gone into the cinema. She wishes she was in there too. She is afraid that if she goes to the windscreen and peers inside, she will see Jake and some girl he regularly sleeps with or has just picked up. And worst of all, he will be laughing too.

Everything goes quiet and then there is a great commotion. The doors fly open. Louie, Sam, Tim and Jake tumble out in a cloud of dope, laughing hysterically.

Still finding his balance, Jake catches her eye. He smiles ruefully.

'Hey bird!' he croaks. 'What are we waiting for?'

'You,' is all she can say. Behind him she sees Tim pulling a mock scowl as if imitating her.

Jake puts his arm around her and they walk ahead of the others.

'They're off their faces,' he says confidentially, a crazed edge in his voice.

'So are you.'

Jake giggles. 'It was all heads. Sam forgot to mention.' He stops and looks at her as though a thought has just struck him. 'Been waiting long?'

'It doesn't matter now.'

After the movie they drop Sam, Louie and Tim off and they are finally alone. It's almost midnight when they pull up in the carpark at the Back Beach. The headlights cut through the darkness and pick out flashes of white foam. When Jake turns off the engine, the muted roar of the ocean takes over. He leans forward on the wheel, his chin resting on his hands. He tells Hannah about his plans with Anton, next full moon. Surfing at night is something he has always wanted to do. To discover what is lost under the blazing sun. In the darkness he would have to surf by ear, by the feel of the ocean and the surge of the waves.

'Like being blind. One sense switched off and the rest on overdrive.' He stares out the windscreen at the blue-black water beyond.

Out of nowhere memories surface. The time he tried to swim the Mersey and was fished out halfway across by the captain of a passing pilot boat. Smells were particularly strong. The tidal salt and the mud flats, the odours of the dockyard, the breweries and margarine factories. Years of pollution had given the water a soft, clinging feel that was strangely comforting. And he wasn't totally blinded. Although it was late in the evening there were the lights of Birkenhead to guide him to the opposite shore.

It was two weeks after his mother's death. He had skipped school and spent the day roaming around the city streets and later, around the docks. He headed up Mount Pleasant and at the top of the hill near the cathedral he stopped and looked around. It was a pockmarked view but he liked it well enough. He had grown up with stories about the bombing during the war and there were still a few blacked-out shells of buildings that stood like memorials to that time. Along with the derelict, boarded-up houses that dotted almost every street, it was in these ruins that Jake and his friends spent most of their spare time. Until that morning at the Royal Liverpool Hospital when his mother slipped into a coma and never woke up again.

After that Jake stayed away from the bombed-out buildings. They were black and crumbling and deserted. What he couldn't understand was where his mother had gone. He remembers walking along the hospital corridor with its chequered, linoleum floor and chrome trolleys glancing past and the sound of moaning in distant rooms. They had come early and at the very moment that they were headed for her room, she was being shifted to intensive care. The nurses were trying to reach Marcus, not realising that he'd already arrived.

Jake ran ahead to her ward, excited because he had a present for her. In woodwork he had made a sphere with the lathe. It was like a little globe of the world, and he had spent hours with sandpaper to get it silky smooth. It felt good in his palm and it was something that his mother could hold on to when she was on her own. He was puffing when he reached her door and had to stop and steady himself. Then he saw her empty bed, the sheets flat and crisp, and not even a dent in the pillow where her head had been. The ball dropped from his hand, bounced once on the floor and rolled off toward the window.

Marcus had warned him that his mother would be leaving them to go on a long journey but Jake had always thought it would be like waving her off at Lime Street Station when she went to London, or at the quayside when she took the ferry across to Ireland to visit her cousins there. Ellen had never gone anywhere without telling him what she was doing and when she'd be back.

When she finally died without saying goodbye, Jake pressed his father for something to hold on to. Where exactly had she gone? Why couldn't they go there too? Marcus struggled for an answer as he looked out the hospital window toward the grey streak of the Mersey. Death was like crossing a river, he said finally, from one world into another. Jake knew about other worlds from

the fairy stories Ellen used to read to him. He knew about
Avalon in the middle of the lake, where all the heroes
went, and about rivers that made people forget who they
were and what they had been. At school he had learnt
that Mersey meant boundary, but the boundary of what?
Jake followed the path of his father's gaze and wondered
what it all meant.

Two weeks later when he was fished from the river,
he was trying to find an answer in the only way he knew
how. Jake worked things out by *doing*. Thinking things
over and trying to solve them that way got him tied up
in knots and only made him feel worse. He had to
experience it for himself. He had spent most of the
afternoon watching the ships being scoured and repaired
in the dry docks. The pier master saw him there, squatting
on the bluestones in his school shorts and socks turned
at the knees, and asked him what he was up to. Jake
knew he couldn't explain, so he said that he wanted to
be a mariner and one day go to sea.

Towards evening Jake wandered down to where the big
liners docked outside the Cunard Building. From there he
marched solemnly to the edge of the quayside and took
off his shoes. As he eased himself over, he noticed that
there was a slimy strip of green weed marking the water
line. It was warmer than he had expected and once he
got his bearings he struck out through the chop toward
the lights on the other side. Death, he had decided, was
something that he could sidle up to and inspect, if he had
the courage to do it. It meant going against all his fears
and forgetting what might lurk in the water ahead. Only

by forcing himself into the darkness could he get close to where his mother had gone.

Jake hasn't spoken for what seems like ages. Hannah looks sideways at him and wonders if he's still stoned.

'Isn't it dangerous, surfing at night?'

He finally stirs. 'Probably. Your peripheral vision is shot. A wave can hit you before you realise it's there.'

'Why take the risk?'

He shrugs as if to say that she couldn't possibly understand. At the same time he seems to be struggling for an answer to the question himself.

Hannah summons up her courage. 'I can think of other things to do at night.'

Jake smiles slowly. His hand comes out of the darkness and rests on her bare arm. His face moves across the space between them. His sun-dried lips are slightly open. Blond stubble glimmers around his mouth. In the instant before he kisses her, she sees his eyelids close like white shutters against his brown skin.

They take it in turns until their clothes are scattered around them in messy pools on the beach house floor. Jake hovers over her, leaning on his hands. He examines the tan-lines that divide her into regions of brown and white. He knows the shape of her body, but not these parts where the sun hasn't reached, where the blue veins run close to the surface and the skin is silky to touch. When they undress side by side at the beach, they always turn the other way.

Each time Jake lifts his head from her mouth, a squat volume of the bible sits at the edge of his vision, like a toad refusing to move. He turns out the light, deliberately blinding them both. They must grope to find one another. Hannah stumbles to the window and raises one of the blinds halfway. He watches her from behind as she reaches for the cord. Her body gone silvery at the edges from the streetlight's glow. Before she can turn around he is standing right behind her.

'Stay,' he whispers as she tries to face him. He lifts her hair and pushes his lips to the back of her neck. As he drags his mouth across her skin, she runs her hands down his flanks and makes his body quiver. Jake is not used to holding back; he has to force himself to slow down. As if reading his thoughts, she drives her teeth into his shoulder, goading him on. He reaches for her mouth and covers it with his own, hungrier than he has ever been.

It's not until his hands move further down her body that she begins to stiffen. She turns around. He lets them drop, expecting her to pull away. Instead she takes his wrist and points to the bedroom. He watches her pick up her clothes and follows her down the hall.

They climb on to the high bed with its cold, starched sheets. It's like being on a stage. Jake wishes they were back on the loungeroom floor. In this room, with its antique wardrobes, oak dressing-table and fancy ceiling, they have become formal and some of the heat has been lost. He wonders if it's her parents' bed.

Hannah starts to talk as they touch and Jake can tell that she is trying to slow the pace. She tells him about a boy in a picture theatre, a stranger who took her hand as if they were in a dream. She tells him of the stories she had spun around him and of her regret that she did not stay.

Jake fingers her, and she grips his cock as she talks, her voice growing thicker as her stories grow more wild. As they roll and laugh in the darkness they begin to understand each other in ways that weren't possible before. Through her words she exposes herself to him, smiling and stripping away her flesh until he can almost see the bone.

Then, in the middle of it, she says something that brings the whole thing to a halt.

Hannah lies alone in the big bed. She puffs the sheet high and watches it fall in a slowly dissolving bubble. She still can't figure out how it happened. He had her so worked up it felt like she could tell him anything and he would understand. With Jake the words just came. God knows where from. Terse, hard-edged words that gave her a feeling of power. 'Gutter language' her mother would have called it. But it was good. It released her from herself. Then one thing led to another and before she knew it, she was on to the events of that evening, the sight of his car rocking, the cries from inside and what she had thought.

It wasn't until she'd finished the story that she noticed the tightening of Jake's grip and the curl of his lip. He entered her silently. Forcefully. Staring down from what seemed like a great height. A snarl on his face. An expression so fierce that she knew she'd never forget it. A torn look.

Afterwards he rolled to one side of her and lay facing

the ceiling. For a time there was just the sound of cars passing on the highway. Then he finally spoke.

'What kind of arsehole do you take me for?'

He stared at her so hard she had to look away. In a quieter, steely voice he kept at her, asking questions. Did she think he would do that to her? Invite her out and then fuck someone before her eyes? Did she really believe he would?

Hannah groaned. That wasn't it, that wasn't what she'd meant.

Jake didn't wait to listen. He had already made up his mind; he knew what was going on. He slapped at a mosquito that had landed on his arm. When he lifted his hand there was a dark star of blood.

'Those nice grammar boys, they wouldn't dream of it, would they? Playing a dirty trick like that. But a surfie bum, a garbo's son drop-out. That's another story. I bet your parents always warned you about types like me.'

There was nothing she could say. He had misunderstood. At the same time, he was right. Even down to her parents' warnings.

He swung off the bed the way he sliced out of a wave, just before the barrel collapsed. He pulled on his jeans and t-shirt, shoved his feet into his runners and walked out. Hannah heard the backdoor slam and footsteps on the concrete path. She waited for the sputter of the engine. She sat up and caught sight of her face in the dressing-table mirror. It was flushed and still puffy with desire. Then the door went again and he was tramping back up the hall.

His car keys had fallen from his pocket.

'Where are they?' he said, glancing around the room as

though she had hidden them from him. There was no anger in his voice now, just tiredness. He spotted them glinting on the floor. He hesitated, then picked them up.

Hannah could see that he had lost interest in storming out a second time. She threw off the blankets and drew him back into bed. He lay there quietly as she unbuttoned his shirt, eased off his jeans and straddled him. They moved together warily this time. Hannah tried not to think about what had just happened. Grey light was seeping through the curtains. Cars were starting up in the street and the birds were making a racket in the eaves. At least they had made it through the night.

When they were done, Jake sat up and lit up a cigarette. Hannah watched the veil of smoke rise up between them as he exhaled. She reached out her hand.

'Give me a drag.'

'You don't smoke.'

'Just once.'

She took it from him and placed her lips where his had been. She managed not to cough.

'I used to have these dreams that I'd started smoking. One drag and I'd be hooked. No control. There were all these temptations out there and you had to resist them, or else.'

Jake managed a smile and butted his cigarette in a vase.

'This time, I really gotta go,' he said, looking out the window.

'Stay for breakfast.'

But he shook his head. He had to meet Louie and Sam at Sphinx.

EIGHT

As HANNAH FINISHES HER late shift, Jake sits in the corner on one of the stools, talking to Ruben. Hannah washes her hands and lifts the long apron over her head feeling immediately lighter. Ruben locks the door behind them and watches them walk up the main street, arms casually slung across each other's backs. As they move off into the darkness Ruben goes to the fusebox and flicks off the lights until the cafe is lit only by the neon insect zapper above the door. The fridge hums into life and there is a drawn-out sizzle as another moth gets fried.

Ruben returns to the window, chews on his moustache and wonders what to do for the rest of the evening. It is just after nine o'clock. Normally he would head for the garage and take out the colored balls to cheer himself up with a few rounds of snooker. Having potted them all for a warm-up, he would empty the pockets and the serious game would begin.

Ruben has always fancied himself in braces and armbands up against Eddie Charlton. When playing alone he circles the table murmuring desultory remarks in a velvety voice like the commentary from *Pot Black*. He has been town champion for so many years that, after a few beers, the idea of playing Eddie Charlton doesn't seem so far-fetched. The only time he feels in command is when he is leaning on the table with a cue in his hand. There is artistry and strategy and grace in this contained world. And the prospect of another win.

Standing in the semi-darkness Ruben follows a large group of young people who have just rolled up at the new Pancake Parlour across the road. Like a set in a western, the floodlit verandah stands out against the night. Unlike Ruben's Cafe, which was built before the building code changed, it has been designed to blend in with the nineteenth-century facades that line the main street. Even Bernie from the Continental, who knows what a threat it poses to Ruben, admitted to being impressed, especially with the bistro menu. 'I think it'll be a winner, Roo,' he said, pausing to let the words sink in. 'You've got to match it.' He didn't say how this was to be done, and just the thought of what it might involve made Ruben feel tired.

Past summers had always been good for Ruben and at first he wasn't too concerned. His fare was basic but it was what people had always wanted on their holidays. He hadn't realised how quickly tastes were changing. When someone asked for a bottle of Perrier he didn't know what it was.

Now Ruben has started to notice that the evening rush is shorter and less frantic, and it's not only because Hannah is there to help him. He has seen families stand in the middle of the road, weighing up the alternatives. The parents, no doubt thinking what Ruben's will cost them, gravitate in his direction while the kids pull the other way. Lately the kids have started winning and now even Jake's mates are defecting. Only six weeks in operation and the

Pancake Parlour is open to 1 am. When the pubs shut at eleven, the party there begins.

After over twenty years in business, the relentlessness of it all is starting to wear Ruben down. He can't even rely on Marie to take his side. She reckons he's got his head in the sand. From every direction the messages are coming at him—move with the times or die.

Ruben blinks at the lights across the road. Everything has gone soft and hazy as though a milky screen has been drawn between him and the world. The Parlour is looking like something out of Walt Disney, and how can he compete with that? He squints through the window wondering if his eyesight is starting to go until he notices that his breath has smudged the glass. He wipes it with his sleeve and marvels at the sight. Still the people keep rolling up until the place is overflowing. There are more of them sitting on the grassy front lawn and the nature strip dividing the road, eating icecreams and enjoying the hot night air.

Ruben has locked his doors just as the town is coming to life.

Hannah and Jake can smell it way before they get there. The last of the diners have left the Fish House restaurant but the side door to the kitchen is thrown wide open. There is laughter above the clatter of pots and pans as though the night were only just beginning. When they reach the lighted doorway, a red face in a chef's hat leans out and thrusts a whole crayfish at them. 'Enjoy!' He laughs at their surprise and before they can say anything, he has ducked back inside and closed the door behind him.

Hannah wraps it in the day's paper, remembering a time she ordered crayfish in a Japanese restaurant. It was still twitching when it landed on the grill. She tells Jake about it, how she couldn't eat it after seeing it die.

Jake spits his gum on the footpath. 'It's very simple. To get meat you have to kill. If you can't face up to that, you're kidding yourself. At least death came quick. Better than watching it happen slowly. Most people don't know what it's like.'

Hannah wants to ask him about it. About his mother. But his voice warns her off.

They continue on through the town and stop at the pub overlooking the Front Beach for some beer to wash down the soft, white flesh. They pass the newly painted bandstand, lit up as if for a show. On the beach, Hannah picks through the remains of the crayfish, then stretches out on the sand, sneaking sideways glances at Jake.

After last week, they're still careful. But Hannah is sure that eventually the words will come. Every second morning they go to the Long Beach together. Jake shows her where the rips are running and which banks are working and explains the finer points of hassling for a wave. On the other mornings, when Hannah works at the cafe, Jake surfs with his mates.

In the stillness the bay might be a giant pond with miniature lights blinking on the other side. Hannah tries to imagine, thousands of years before, when there was no bay. Just the Yarra flowing out through the Rip.

'Strange to think of it all exposed. Open country. I wonder what's been submerged.'

Jake tells her about the dredging to salvage the Front Beach. Last summer, he adds with a grin, tourists lay on sand that, only weeks before, had lined the bottom of the bay.

As he speaks, two fishermen wade in through the shallows toward the beach. There is the swish of the water against their legs and the occasional cool splash as their buckets hit the surface.

Hannah starts to undress. 'Coming?' She doubts it. He thinks swimming in the bay is for families.

She runs across the sand. The water isn't cold but the inkiness of it makes her shiver. As it gets deeper, she tries not to think of the darkness opening up beneath her, a darkness dense with life.

Near the jetty pylons she sees flashes of movement. The flowery shape of a baby squid and a sudden constellation of others drifting off into the blackness. Breast-stroking smoothly she glides after them until the curses of the fishermen reach her. Hannah ducks under the water and is pushing back to the shore when she collides with something hard.

She surfaces with a gasp. Jake has come in after all.

Back on the beach the warm air folds around them like a blanket, and within minutes they might never have been in the water. They talk about the hot spell and wonder when it will end. In the air-conditioned cafe it was bearable, but whenever Hannah stepped outside it hit her like a blast from the outback. During the day the roads went soft and the nights seemed becalmed.

On their way back to the highway, they pass an outside shower attached to a toilet block. Hannah gives Jake her things.

'Hold on,' she says.

'It'll make you hotter.'

'What?'

'The salt on your skin. It keeps you cool.'

'How?' she laughs, remembering her chemistry lessons. It doesn't sound right.

Jake sucks in his cheeks.

'Forget it.'

The look on his face says it all. The ease between them is gone. Jake is digging a crater in the path with his toes. Hannah can hear the scraping of his nails against the baked ground.

'Maybe you're right. Maybe it's bullshit,' he says still staring at the dirt.

'I didn't say that.'

'It's just something I've noticed in winter. After a surf the salt keeps you cold.'

Hannah struggles for an explanation. Salt can make the skin clammy but it has to dissolve to have a cooling effect. She's thinking this over, wondering what to say, when she realises that Jake has left her behind.

She can see the back of him moving along the road, a white towel slung around his neck. She catches up and turns him to face her, pressing her tongue to his mouth. It tastes of the sea. She feels him respond and knows nothing needs to be said. She takes his hand and they walk back along the highway, the whole night stretching ahead of them.

NINE

EVERY AFTERNOON MARCUS WORKS in the dunes planting marram grass and spinifex to stop the sand from blowing away. From a distance the coastline looks rugged and invincible but up close it crumbles at his touch. Day and night rivulets of sand trickle down the pockmarked, sandstone face. Slowly, the cliffs are dissolving. It's not only the wind, sea spray and waves that wear it away, but the plucking and drilling of tiny marine animals—periwinkles, barnacles and mussels—living on the pitted, biscuity surface. Sometimes the changes are dramatic. Just months ago, a minor landslide at the Back Beach saw a chunk of the cliff slide abruptly into sea.

Marcus straightens. His back aches from the constant bending and his eyes are stinging from the glare. He wonders if he's starting to hallucinate. Figures in strange clothes are heading towards him across the ridged hummocks of the dunes. He looks again. Two men in wide hats and ponchos, and a woman in a peasant skirt. They wave madly and run towards him as though he is the first human they have sighted in days. They are Japanese. Tourists in Mexican dress who want him to take their photo. They smile sheepishly and arrange themselves as if taking a siesta, brandishing guns, drinking Tequila. After much bowing, they continue on their way.

Marcus is too stunned to tell them they shouldn't be there. He has just erected a series of signs: RECLAMATION AREA. NO ENTRY. He doesn't like keeping people out. But too much damage has been done. The dunes are the soft flesh covering the bare bones of the foreshore. Blowouts are his biggest worry, the sudden ravaging that strips the land back to the ice age, breaking it into gravel like the stony tracts of the Sahara. He knows that it's only a salvage job but halting the drifting dunes has brought a satisfaction he couldn't have imagined. When high winds whip up the sand in spirals and carry it out over the ocean or inland toward the city, he is seized by a terrible urgency. Every patch he can secure with mesh and grass is a small victory against time and loss.

A narrow spit of land looms, rigid and vulnerable. Thrust from the ochre cliffs, the worn face of the Sphinx watches its approach. As the ocean floor begins to shelve, the liquid shock wave compresses and has nowhere to go but up.

When the Mexicans have disappeared, Marcus returns to his work. The sun scalds the top of his hat. He digs and plants. It still amazes him that anything can grow in this desiccated soil, buffeted by the salt spray and the endless wind. He admires the hardiness of the grasses that can survive and secure the shifting terrain. He can't stop worrying about Jake. Over the past year there's been a brittleness about him, as if he is about to snap at any time. Marcus has given up asking about his plans or trying to organise him a job.

Marcus often wonders if he should have been stricter.

Not long after his wife's death Jake came home from school with a stud in his ear. He wasn't Johnnie any more, he announced. He was Jake. 'Jake' was tough and sharp, it had a rakish ring. It made Marcus think of the underworld, of crims and con men, and he hoped it was a passing fad. He tried to talk him out of it. If Johnnie was too boyish what about Jack? Jack and the Beanstalk, Jack the Giant Killer. Jack was a good, solid name. Johnnie shook his head. 'Sure, like Jack and Jill. No way.' After that he wouldn't answer to anything other than Jake.

Gathering up his tools, Marcus goes back to the Parks' hut for his tea-break. Jake had said he would drop by but Marcus wasn't going to hold him to it. He hasn't seen his son for over a week. Sometimes, Marcus wonders why Jake doesn't just move out and be done with it, instead of coming and going like he can't make up his mind.

Marcus is getting ready to leave when Jake finally rolls up. Jake tells him he can't stay. He just wants to make sure Marcus will be at the pub that evening. There's someone he wants him to meet.

Marcus can tell from his manner that Jake is excited. Much as he tries to sound casual, there is pride in the way he speaks of this girl from the city.

Hannah watches the barman pulling a beer, the foamy head flowing down the sides of a glass. He places it on a strip of towel that stretches the length of the bar. A hand reaches out and takes hold of it. A cheer goes up around the television. The drone of the race call builds to a pitch. A rapid fire of words that usually drives her insane, but tonight she lets it swirl around her. She is content to sit at the bar with Jake, their elbows touching, and wait for Marcus to come.

Hannah is tearing open a packet of nuts when a voice calls out to Jake. She is surprised that Marcus is so young. Early forties perhaps, and with dreadlocks. Jake swings around frowning, then lets out a hoot of surprise. Hannah watches them embrace and realises who it is.

Anton gives Hannah a brief nod then turns back to Jake.

'Man, look at this,' he says. From his combat-green pack he draws out a fist full of grains and lets them fall slowly to the bar. A small pyramid forms. He leans across and grins.

'Gold dust. Cactus gold.'

His voice is husky, extravagant, ironic.

Jake had told Hannah all about Cactus, the surfer's Eldorado this side of the West Australian border. He spoke of it like a legend. And now Anton had stepped right out of it, larger-than-life, having driven twenty hours straight.

'So what's the go?' Anton says.

'Nothing much,' Jake says, avoiding Hannah's eyes. He tells him they're waiting for Marcus. He doesn't say anything about Hannah. He acts like nothing has changed, but Anton isn't fooled.

'The big introduction.'

Jake just laughs and orders more beers.

Hannah stares at the floor while they talk. Or, while Anton talks and Jake listens. The colors of the carpet clash.

It hadn't bothered her before. All around her everyone's getting pissed. She notices the sickly smell of spilt beer and stale cigarettes. Men with ruddy faces are talking boozily to their mates without ever finishing a sentence. Already the night's slipping away.

After two pots Anton is in his stride. He has just hit the Eyre Highway and the desert calls. From here it's a matter of driving straight and staying awake. To keep his mind sharp he counts wildlife killed on the road and blasts his horn to scare off the crows. Finally he spots the grey funnels of Penong's wheat silos and he knows he's almost there.

Anton pauses at this crucial moment and sips his beer.

At this rate, Hannah thinks, it'll take all night. Anton has not met her eye once since he began to speak and Jake seems to have forgotten she's there. She catches sight of her face in the mirror behind the bar. A pair of black, angry eyes. But she's determined not to let it show. She reaches out her hand and strokes the back of Jake's neck.

'Another beer? My shout.'

His body stiffens under her touch. He shoots her a dark look. The message is clear. Hands off in front of Anton.

Anton finishes his cigarette and crushes the butt with his thumb.

'The turn-off at Penong is something else.'

He looks hard at Jake.

'You're driving across a salt pan. A whole series of 'em. Foam at the edges. The road's dead straight and it disappears. Just these low, red shrubs here and there. Everything else is white. Twenty kilometres of it. Then, in the distance these dunes on the horizon. But they might be a mirage. It's not till you're right up close that you can tell. You drive over a ridge and suddenly it's there in front of you. These amazing waves.'

Not one for rushing a story, Anton is still setting the scene when Marcus arrives. He is a short man in his early fifties with a weathered face and sandy, thinning hair. Hannah has a feeling she has seen him before. The likeness to Jake is remarkable. The same blue-green eyes, only slightly faded; the same lightning-flash smile. He stands with his arm proudly around Jake's shoulders and nods hello. Then he pulls a stool up next to Hannah.

'Jake says you're at the university.'

There is a touch of awe in the way he says 'university', spelling out each syllable. Hannah is struck by his accent, which is much stronger than his son's. It makes Liverpool seem suddenly close. Hannah's father often spoke of going to England, but it was the south that he had in mind. The university towns of Oxford and Cambridge, the Lake District, the Roman ruins of Bath. For years he had been subscribing to *Country Life* with its endless pages of stately homes and articles about grouse hunting. Some evenings, after preparing his sermon, he would sit in his study with the hard bound volume, *The Road Maps of England* and stroll down country lanes he would never visit. The England in his head was secure and unchanging like the photographs in *Country Life*, and he wanted to keep it that way.

'I was,' Hannah says, wondering if she has made a mistake. She tells him she has dropped out.

'That's a real shame.'

'You sound like my parents,' she smiles. She remembers

that she had promised to call them that evening. They worry about her being on her own. 'I can always go back.'

Hannah would rather change the subject. She glances over her shoulder. Anton and Jake are killing themselves laughing. She turns back to Marcus who is looking at her with concern. He has sized things up.

He leans forward, speaking in confidence.

'Anton likes an audience. He's used to having Jake to himself.'

He pats her hand.

'First things first,' he says, turning to Jake and Anton. 'Let's grab a table, boys. We're up here like birds on a wire.'

Once they have settled at a table, Marcus stares across at his son with a tight smile. Jake is shifting in his chair. Hannah tries to get his attention but he might as well be on the moon. Marcus looks like he's about to pounce.

'I can't stay long, son. Starting at five,' he says.

'Don't let me keep you up.'

'You're not,' he says losing his patience. 'I've been talking to Hannah. She tells me she goes jogging. I think I've seen her at London Bridge.'

Hannah wishes she wasn't there.

No one speaks for a long time. Marcus fixes his gaze on his son. Suddenly Anton says breezily, 'So how's old Ruben these days?'

Jake jumps on the question. 'Still threatening to sell.' He explains about Marie and the restaurant opposite.

Marcus downs his beer.

'I give up,' he says to Hannah. 'I'm sorry, I've got to go.' To Jake he says in a hard voice, 'I'll see you later.'

He is out the door. Hannah can see him passing the window as he strides down the dark street. She stands and pulls her jacket off the back of the chair. It was a night that was best forgotten.

'See you Friday,' she says.

Jake casually takes her aside. He fidgets for a moment before coming out with it. He can't make it Friday and perhaps not next week either. Anton has plans for a trip down the west coast.

He lowers his voice. 'Anton's been gone a long time.' He takes her by the shoulders and quickly kisses her forehead. 'Don't be mad,' he pleads.

Hannah shrugs, her throat so tight no words will come. Only the night before they were lying on her bed, beneath the poster of the perfect wave, talking about the rest of the summer. Just when they'd worked things out, the ground had shifted again.

For some reason Hannah can't feel angry. Not with Jake. She is too aware of Anton's power. She'd like to pick up her glass and fling it against the wall. Just to hear it smash. Instead, she stares coldly at Anton and walks away.

TEN

THE RAIN IS HEAVY when they reach the boom gates of the army barracks. Marie pulls the car over. She's about to wind down the window when a soldier leans out of the booth. He peers through the windscreen, breaks into a knowing smile and waves them on. The boom gates lift and Marie drives past, her lips pressed together, her eyes straight ahead. When they're out of sight, she looks across at Hannah and they both start rocking, helpless with laughter.

Since the early days of settlement, the tip of the Peninsula has been off limits. At first it was an army fort and a quarantine station. For almost a century, ships sailing under the yellow flag would dock with their febrile cargo. Recently it had become an officer training camp but was still closed to the public.

Hannah and Marie had planned to spend the day at the beach but the rain put an end to that, and they wound up playing minigolf. Just ahead of them on the course two young officers were talking about their girlfriends who were to visit them that afternoon. One of the officers was concerned about the rules but his friend brushed his worries aside. The gatekeeper had been worded up to let the girls through. They slapped hands American style and quickly finished their game, then drove off toward the barracks. An hour later, Hannah and Marie pulled up at the boom gates.

The rain is easing off. As the road rises out of the scrub they can see the ocean on one side, and the bay on the other.

'I don't believe it,' Hannah says when she can finally speak. 'What happens when the *real* girlfriends turn up?'

The tyres sizzle over the wet bitumen. Marie takes a hand off the wheel and pats Hannah's thigh.

'Hannah, Hannah, Hannah. They can only throw us out. Lighten up.'

But for Hannah it's not that easy. For almost twenty years the Point has been forbidden territory. The only people she knows who go there are surfers, who either climb around the rocky shoreline to Spooks or take a motor boat to Quarantine Station at the mouth of the bay.

One day Jake was out at Spooks when some officers were practising in the rifle range. They spotted the surfers and lined up like a firing squad along the top of the cliff. One of the soldiers had a loud hailer and told them to clear off. When the order was ignored, they raised their guns and pretended to take aim. Jake was determined to call their bluff but Louie panicked and grabbed an on-coming wave that delivered him straight onto the rocks. When Jake and the others reached the shore they found him sitting on the sand, his head in his hands and his hair matted with blood.

This was what happened at the Point. It was a place where sailing ships were wrecked and lives lost, and where one summer day when Hannah was five years old, a prime minister had drowned. If a prime minister could disappear before the eyes of his minders then it seemed that anything could happen. The power of State was nothing to the forces of Bass Strait.

Hannah jumps when she hears the sound of a motor behind them. A green army vehicle has come out of nowhere.

'Shit,' she groans. She wonders if they are carrying guns and whether they will order them out and frisk them.

To their right, in a grassy clearing, are the officers' quarters. The buildings are limestone. Colonial, with wide verandahs. An outpost of civilisation. In the distance a column of men and women in uniform march towards a flag pole.

The car seems to be gaining on them.

'We shouldn't have come,' Hannah is saying. 'I knew it.'

Marie slows down and is pulling on to the gravel when she glances in the rear vision mirror. The road behind them is empty. The car has turned off at the barracks and has disappeared into the tea-tree.

She grins at Hannah. 'I thought they had us.'

'Me too.' But Hannah's not laughing.

Marie leans on the accelerator and turns the radio up full blast, filling the car with opera. She opens the window and sings along as the music gains momentum. Her red and white scarf fluttering around her neck.

'Why haven't I done this before? Don't answer that.'

Hannah looks out the window wishing she could share Marie's mood. She hasn't seen her like this before. There is a hard brightness about her now. Like she finally knows what she wants.

Steam rises off the road ahead. The clouds are breaking

up as the view before them widens. There are moments when they can see clear to the Heads and the lighthouse on the opposite point. Somewhere over there, on the highway along the coast, Jake's old Holden is moving further and further west. As the music swells, Hannah closes her eyes and tries to go with it, banishing all those thoughts. Through her eyelids she senses the changing light. The horizon shrinks as the sun is obscured and opens out again when the cloud passes.

The road stops at the old fort, or what is left of it. They climb over the ruined walls and down the cliff to the crescent of beach at the point. Hannah has seen it from across the bay. She can't quite believe she is on the spot that had always been out of reach. In her mind it will always be at a distance. The wind is blustery but the Rip looks surprisingly tame. She's disappointed there are no motor boats, tankers or yachts against which to measure the flow of the tide.

Taking off her shoes, she wades cautiously into the water, pulling her skirt up around her waist. The cold edges up her calves. The bay is to her right, to her left, the Strait. Here where they meet head on she'd hoped for some sign of collision, turbulence. Some sign of the commotion the fishermen had told her about. One of them drove a pilot boat until the Rip got the better of him. He reckoned the name said it all. Some rite of passage. But today it's keeping its secrets close. There's nothing to see but fluffy white caps whipped up by the easterly wind.

Jake says reading the tides is a skill that takes years. When they touch each other, everything's understood. It's strange to know the intimate things and yet be in the dark about so much. Surely there are ways of understanding the rest. It's too lonely otherwise. But what more can Jake know about her when she's almost a stranger to herself?

Hannah runs her fingertips over the water as she moves out. Her legs are dragged forward. She almost loses her footing as the water swirls up her thighs and higher, driving out to the ocean. With every step the pull grows stronger, the seafloor falls away.

Above the sound of the ocean and the seagulls crying, a voice is calling her name. A tuneful sing-song like children playing hidey. But now the tune is changing. An urgent staccato that jolts her out of her daze. Only when she looks back does it hit her. The distance to the shore and the grip of the tide. She turns slowly against the invisible tug, her whole body resisting its force. With slow, dream-like steps she makes her way back to the beach.

Only from the top of the cliff does Hannah notice those unseen currents and telling patterns on the surface.

Marie is sitting in the car eating a sandwich. She looks cross. Hannah opens the door and climbs in.

'That was dumb,' Marie says, still chewing.

'I wanted to see how far I could go.'

'You picked a great place for it.' She looks at her friend, her voice softens. 'What were you doing out there?'

'I told you,' she almost snaps.

'If it's anything to do with Jake, get a hold of yourself. Jake's not free. Don't think you can sort him out.'

Hannah turns angrily to her friend.

'I don't *want* to sort him out. I like him the way he is.'

They drive back in silence until they reach a small

cemetery near the Quarantine Station where the drowned and the fevered are buried. Those who never made it. Many of the graves are mounds of earth with small, eroded tablets for headstones. The saddest are the family graves, granite slabs surrounded by rust-colored, wrought-iron fencing.

Marie stretches out on the sun-warmed tombstone of Jemma Pike, second daughter of James and Annie Pike, born 1857, died 1861. She watches Hannah roaming around, inspecting the graves and wonders who Jemma might have become if she'd had the chance. Hannah stops and sits by Marie, pulling at some weeds that have sprouted from a crack in the tomb.

'Is Ruben alright?'

'What do you mean?'

'Yesterday, after you left for town, he didn't speak. For the whole day. Just grunted if I asked him something. Like it was beyond him to form a sentence. He was holding himself together. But only just.'

Marie is staring at the sky. A cloud drifts across the sun and sends a shadow racing over the ground toward them. Ruben had never trusted words. They were tools of his trade, a way of fooling people. He was still working door-to-door when they married. In the evenings he came home and sat in his favorite chair and didn't speak for at least an hour. He'd grown to hate the sound of his voice. Marie could understand that. The need for silence after trying to flog cleaners all day. She didn't mind his silence then. He was a thoughtful man and only spoke when he had something to say.

Perhaps he'd just run out of things to say. Or perhaps

there didn't seem to be a point to conversation any more. It frightened her, that it had come to this. But what frightened her more was the thought of another twenty-five years like the last, of a deepening silence. Like most couples, they had a shorthand communication. Things understood without being said. A look, a raised eyebrow, a private joke. The rituals that bound them together. But somewhere along the way these gestures had lost currency, become a dead language. Like Latin or Ancient Greek.

If they could've had it out, it might have been different. If they could've fought and shouted and told each other what was on their minds. If only Ruben could bring himself to say it, say what a hard bitch she'd become. Then she could round on him with accusations of her own, knowing there was some truth to it—that her heart *had* hardened against him.

Eventually Marie says, 'He gets like that. You know what's going on.'

'I've got an idea.'

'I saw a solicitor. It's horrible. But there's no other way out.'

Hannah doesn't know what to say. She has grown to like Ruben with his taciturn air, his furtive questions and his flashes of dry humor. She doesn't want to take sides. A cold war is going on and she would rather not be witnessing it. She isn't used to seeing people break up. It's always been something that happened to strangers.

'I guess you've made up your mind.' Hannah tries not to sound grudging. She thinks she can imagine what Ruben must feel.

Marie gets up and brushes the dirt from the back of her slacks. There's a narrow track through the tea-tree scrub running down to the bay. She can see a wedge of yellow and blue in the distance.

'I guess I have.'

Dolphins play in the ferry's wake, water shattering from their backs as they leap and dive. Two children run down the deck squealing with delight. At the stern they stand rapt at the sight, their small eyes darting and bodies straining against the sea rail, longing to dive overboard and frolic too.

Jake settles into a deckchair and watches them. Dolphins are nothing special. He sees them all the time out surfing. One morning at Quarantine he thought he'd met his first shark. He saw a fin ride up through the foam and a grey shadow beneath. It kept coming at him as he sat on his board, unable to move. Then its snout poked through the surface. As it flipped out of the wave he was sure he heard it laughing.

But the first time he saw a dolphin, he was fresh from Liverpool and he was thrilled, just like those kids. It's getting harder to find thrills in things like that. The waves need to be bigger, the manoeuvres more radical, the risks always greater. It makes him feel old beyond his years. And yet when he sees Hannah scrabbling for a wave—her eyes wide and uncertain as the water swells beneath her before it pitches her down the face—flashes of pleasure return.

To his amazement he has something to teach her. Anton had always been the one with the advice and knowledge and the ability to pass it on. Jake was impatient with Hannah at first. He told her she'd have to work it out for herself. Then he realised there were basic things she had no idea about, and that he could easily set her right. Sometimes he hears himself explaining things he didn't know he knew. Or things he didn't think he had the words for. He is constantly surprising himself. He has seen her struggling for a wave, looking all but done when suddenly something will click and his words become her actions.

The Peninsula is tapering away. A light drizzle is starting to fall. The waxy smell of engine fuel mingles with the salt spray. Everything is grey and damp. Jake hadn't pictured it like this when they discussed it in the pub last night. He had imagined sun, heat and blue skies and the road stretching out ahead. That's how it was in Anton's stories of Cactus and the desert and the sheer cliffs of the Great Australian Bight.

He takes the stairs down below to escape the rain. Anton is sprawled out on a row of seats, snoring lightly. The ferry is almost empty. He wonders what Hannah's doing. She would be at work by now. Sometimes he slips into the shop unseen so that he can sit by the aspidistra and watch her like he did at the start. He knows her ways by now—her cautious smile with the customers, her concentration when she counts out their change, her fingers toying with her necklace as she says goodbye. He likes it when she talks to the men, especially when they make her laugh. He studies the curve of her mouth and her serious eyes and wonders what's going on behind them.

Anton is stirring. Jake can feel his eyes following him as he wanders aimlessly around the cabin.

'Forget her,' he says sleepily. 'She'll be there when you get back.'

Jake shoves his hands into the pockets of his coat and pulls a face.

Anton tries again. 'She knows the deal. Relax.'

Jake doesn't want to be reminded of last night. He wishes Anton hadn't brought it up. All he wants to do is to get on the road and drive. Leave everything behind. He has been waiting too long for Anton to get crabby with him now. He goes and sits in the car and listens to the radio until the ferry docks.

As they drive along the winding Great Ocean Road, Jake tries to recall the way things looked when he was thirteen years old and on his first surf trip down this coast. Anton was his guide and nothing since has matched it. It wasn't like the Peninsula. Here you could see the coast rolling out before you as you drove along—inlets, beach breaks and monumental outcrops. They would stop where the surf looked good and when the sea breeze sprang up in the evenings they would set up camp on the foreshore. Usually they ate from a tin, then Anton played his guitar.

Often, when they sat in the dark, the red coals of the fire at their feet, Anton would elaborate his theories about the decline of surfing culture. He liked to talk of the way things were when surfing was natural, like the flow of the tide and the wave, the morning calm and the afternoon breeze. Outside the rat-race. Like an art. Just living in the moment. Competition was fucking up the spirit of surfing. Instead of being a communion between the self and the sea it had become like everything else.

Anton said people had it all wrong. The only competition that mattered was the one with yourself. He encouraged Jake to believe he didn't need to compete. Everyone could see that Jake was hot. There was no need to prove it. He could still win people's respect without selling out. *That* was the true art of surfing.

It wasn't difficult for Jake to be persuaded by Anton. He still remembered what it was like when he was serious about diving. Once the pressure was on to compete and train, all the fun went; it lost its point. Besides, the future was too remote to worry about. Jake imagined it unrolling before him like a coastline without end.

It wasn't until Anton went away to Cactus, that it finally hit Jake with any force. He was going nowhere. Anton had taken the plot of Jake's future with him, and without him nothing made any sense. Only Anton could tell the story the way Jake needed to hear it. Only Anton could make it end the way it should. To everyone else Jake was just a good surfer who'd missed his chance.

Jake is thinking this over as they take the dusty turn-off to Bells Beach. Clouds of red swirl up as they skid across dried up puddles and judder over the corrugations, almost veering into the scrub. A stream of cars with boards strapped to their roofs passes them, heading the other way.

'Looks like bad news,' Anton says, winding up the window.

Jake doesn't answer. He has red cliffs and glassy waves

fixed in his mind. The surf has to be good because he has something he wants to show Anton. He has been telling him about his latest aerial manoeuvre, it takes him right out of the wave, arcing through the air and floating back across the lip to re-enter the open face. He wants Anton to photograph him.

When they get to the carpark they can see why the mass exodus. Whatever is driving the swell has dished up something big and the south-easterly is turning it nasty. Row after row of massive close-outs. No neatly peeling waves in that famous bowl, but big jaws of foam snapping shut in one go. Even the shorebreak is hazardous.

Anton places his tripod at the top of the cliff and says he'll be down as soon as he has got some shots. Jake stands on the beach for a while looking for the best point of entry and launches himself in. As he struggles with the dumpers he remembers how helicopters had been used during competitions when the shorebreak got too big. The competitors would be flown to the other side of the break and dropped, and Jake can understand why.

When he finally makes it out there, everyone else has gone in and the conditions are getting worse. He tries a few risky take-offs and pays for it badly. During a severe wipe-out he is struck on the head by his board. He comes up dizzy to find the world gone blurry and another set steaming towards him. After two frustrating hours of being churned up and spat out, he lets the whitewater ferry him to shore.

Anton is sitting crossed-legged on the top of the cliff, shaking his head, his camera packed away.

ELEVEN

HANNAH THROWS BACK HER head. Her breath is rapid and shallow. She slows to a crawl. The soft-faced boy is skipping along sideways like a crab, trying to talk. Hannah can't remember his name. She had slipped into an easy rhythm that made her forget she was actually running. Then he had come bounding down from the club house and broken the spell.

'You haven't been round lately,' he is saying. 'I thought you'd gone home. But here you are.'

Hannah stares at him. 'I didn't know I was under surveillance.'

He grins and falls into a jog at her side. 'Have you been sick or something?'

'Sick?'

'You stopped running.'

'I was doing other things.' She remembers his name now. Fraser. He was a face she used to see at the bus stop and the occasional inter-school dance. His father is a politician and his family have one of those houses overlooking the bay. Any moment now, she fears, he will say something about the 'girls' school' and she will be sucked back in time. Shrink back into that girl in the checked uniform, boater hat and starched blazer with the prefect's badge on the lapel. She has the urge to sprint away.

'Weren't you a swimmer?' He is studying her shoulders.

'Not really.'

'But you like to keep fit. You look after your body. I can see that. You should join the club.'

There is a blitheness about him, an ability to ignore what he doesn't want to hear.

'Why should I do that?'

'You save lives. Not many people can say that. Makes you feel good.'

Hannah looks at the water. For the last few days there's been nothing but on-shore winds chopping up a large swell.

'I'd be lucky to save myself.'

He tells her how they teach survival skills. Most people don't recognise the dangers. They're blind. They step into a rip without knowing it's there. 'You've got to learn how to read the ocean.'

Fraser can see that he's got her attention. He tells her about the training program at the club the following week. An intensive course. Then she could go for her Bronze. 'Everyone bunks up here.'

Hannah smiles weakly. No way. Too much like a school camp. But she's thinking fast. If she can use her head, why do it the hard way? By the time Jake gets back she will be on her feet.

Fraser breaks into her thoughts. 'Jeremy and Georgia are doing it too.'

'Those two?' Hannah looks at him incredulously.

'Amazing isn't it?' Fraser says lowering his voice, but looking pleased with himself. 'They'd rather be out on the yacht, but I got them to see the benefits.'

At London Bridge she turns back and jogs the way she came, wondering what he means by 'benefits'. When they reach the club house she tells him she'll give it some thought.

'After the training, you go on patrol,' he says eagerly. 'Tell the rubber necks where to go.'

Hannah is surprised by his sudden vehemence. 'The rubber necks?'

'Surfers. Dope heads. They get between the flags, we piss them off.'

Hannah remembers hearing Jake talk of the 'clubbies' with the same kind of disdain. The whole plan is starting to look misguided.

'It's not for me,' she says, starting to move off.

Fraser comes after her.

'Hey, forget all that.' He grins and leaps in front of her running backwards. 'Say you'll think about it and I'll leave you alone.'

Hannah finds herself laughing again. He's the kind of person it's hard to stay annoyed with. A numbers man like his father. There must be factions in the club.

Hannah doesn't really care about his reasons. She has reasons of her own. She weighs up the risks. The risk of antagonising Jake and the risk of the sea itself. Half an hour later she is at the cafe, showering before work. By the time she's dressed and behind the counter, her mind's made up.

Over the next week the swell suddenly drops away to nothing, leaving them mucking about in half-metre mush for days on end. Then the rain comes down and there is nothing else to do but play cards and drink in the tent. One morning when Jake swims up from the murk of a heavy sleep his bones are aching and waves of nausea keep threatening to swamp him.

Anton is already up.

'We gotta get out of here or I'll go nuts,' he says.

Jake sinks back into his rubber mattress. 'Where to?'

'Johanna.'

Just the thought of it exhausts him. Jake doesn't think he can move. He seems to have caught some kind of flu.

'I feel like I'm burning up.'

Anton is unmoved. Jake isn't getting out of it that easily.

Jake rolls over and stares at Anton wondering if he has heard right. 'Get out of what?'

'You wanted the shots, man.'

There is an edge to Anton's voice that Jake hasn't heard before. He is about to protest when Anton adds, 'You wanna go back, don't you? You wanna go back for a fuck.'

For the first time it occurs to Jake that Anton might be jealous. 'This is for real,' he says wearily. He just wants to sleep.

Anton puts his hand to Jake's forehead then dives into his pack. 'Take these. Give it ten minutes.' He tips four white tablets into Jake's palm.

Jake swallows and waits. Slowly he eases himself up to his feet and starts pulling on his jeans.

They continue down the coast stopping only for food. Neither of them speak. Anton does all the driving and Jake lies flat out in the back seat with his feet propped up on the opposite door. The scenery flashes by like an endless, silent film. Slowly it goes out of focus and Jake loses track of where they are. As they pass through the Otways, everything darkens as the trees and giant ferns block out the light. They seem to be heading underwater, diving steeply away from the surface. Colors start to go—red first. When Jake knocks his hand, it oozes green blood. Yellows disappear from the spectrum until there is only blue. Then finally, utter darkness. Grotesque, deep sea creatures flit by—luminescent viper and anglerfish whose inner organs flash messages through the gloom. Still in control at the wheel, Anton points them ever deeper as water seeps in through the cracks. Jake tells him they've got to turn back but Anton just shakes his head. They are right on course, he says.

It's late afternoon when Jake is woken abruptly from his feverish sleep. He hears the engine cut out and the door slam. He sits bolt upright, looks around and then scrambles after Anton. They leave the Holden in the camping ground and walk across the barren dunes. An onshore wind whips at their hair in savage gusts. The coast is totally exposed. Here the ocean swell travels unimpeded through deep water before hitting the land with the force of a head-on collision.

Anton takes one look and shakes his head. Jake is leaning on his shoulder relishing the wind.

'Forget it,' Anton says. 'Looks like we're out of luck.'

Jake peers at the grey, churning water. He feels like

laughing. A crazy hysterical urge is welling up inside. A smack in the face from a cold wave is just what he needs.

He tells Anton to get his camera ready.

'You're off your head. You're not going out there.'

Jake turns to him, his brain now as feverish as his body. He didn't know there was so much resentment in him. This time Anton is not going to stop him.

'Just watch me.'

All he needs is one good wave for that sequence of shots—his proof that the maneouvre can work. His evidence to show the world that he is up there with the best. Most of all, he wants to see how it looks. To have some image of himself.

Anton has his arms folded across his chest. 'It's ten foot and closing out. This morning you could hardly get out of bed. Think about it man. You'll get eaten.'

Jake can feel the pressure on his windpipe from his swollen glands. He swallows hard. He unhooks the octopus straps that secure the boards to the roof-racks and rubs in the wax, sweat trickling down behind his ears. He is pulling on his wetsuit when a giddy spell comes over him and he has to lean against the car. Everything is seesawing around him like he is already out in the water.

He has just managed to straighten up when Anton appears from behind. Jake spins around but moves too fast and his whole body crumbles as if he had no bones. He tries to get up but the effort is too much. He rests his forehead on the sand while gathering his strength. The next thing he knows Anton is heaving him up by the armpits and draping him over his shoulder. His toes drag across the ground and then he is flat out on the back seat, his nose pressed into the vinyl.

Towards evening Marcus is driving through the main street on his way home. The shopping centre is quiet. Ahead of him the bay is spread out like a silver tray. Apart from the elegance of the limestone buildings and grand old hotels, what had attracted him to this spot was its position. It's a town with the sea at the end of almost every street. The bay, the Rip and the Strait. An open vista wherever he looked.

Growing up in a shipping port had meant always knowing there was a way out. An escape route. All arterial roads into the city lead to the Mersey at Pierhead. When Marcus was a child, everyone dreamed of going to sea on a merchant ship but Marcus was happiest just looking out across the water. It was enough to have the ocean there at hand always promising something more, like a puzzle that could never be solved. He liked to gather the clues it tossed up. His territory was that shifting zone where the land and water met.

As usual he stops at the Continental for a beer. Most days he drinks at the public bar but the warm evening draws him outside to where the tourists sit under the umbrellas on the footpath. A young couple at the next table are drinking white wine and eating antipasto. The man leans forward as he talks, holding his glass mid-air. There is something about the woman who is sitting back watching him—her solemn gaze and the way she holds her head to one side—that makes him think of Hannah.

The first thing that struck him about her, that night they met at the pub, was the way she sat up so straight on the stool, looking alert. He could tell she wasn't used to being in public bars. On her way back from the Ladies, Hannah moved awkwardly through the crowded room as if she'd just put on a new skin. Marcus had been surprised at first. She couldn't be more different from Jake. He guessed that was part of the attraction, but how much did she really know about his son?

Two skateboarders are weaving in and out of the verandah posts. Marcus watches them swoop on to the road before mounting the curb to negotiate the posts once more, and doesn't notice Hannah's approach. Suddenly she's beside him, smiling as though she has just stepped out of his thoughts. She is holding a butcher's paper package like a swaddled child. It's steaming from the top, rich with the smell of deep fried batter and fish. He remembers the first time he saw her when she was running along the beach. She was almost upon him when he felt the shudder of her steps and looked up startled, just as he was doing now.

He pulls up one of the white plastic chairs. Hannah offers him a chip. She wants to know if he has heard from Jake. Jake had called her once from a phonebox, she says, somewhere down the coast but the line was bad. He had sounded a long way off and his voice got drowned by the cars and trucks passing on the highway. There hadn't been time for him to say where he was because the coins ran out and he didn't call back.

Hannah rips the butcher's paper and spreads the contents out before them. Seagulls mill about, their white-rimmed eyes watching every move.

Marcus has heard nothing from Jake and he doesn't expect to. Whenever he thinks of his son he gets a tight, helpless feeling in his chest.

'Don't worry about Jake,' he says, more to reassure himself than Hannah. 'Jake can look after himself.'

Hannah licks her fingers and smiles across at him. Marcus is glad of her company. Glad that she has sought him out, if only to talk about Jake. Too much of his time is spent alone. Lately he has been whispering to his shells as he cleans and polishes them. The larger ones he puts to his ear, straining above the distant whoosh for the faintest promise of a voice.

Marcus studies the crazed surface of his hands, aware of his age. He wonders how he must look to her. He must be as old as her father, the clergyman.

A clergyman's daughter. Hannah laughs uneasily when he calls her this. He can tell she doesn't like it but she's too polite to say. She doesn't want to be known as anyone's daughter. It ties her to a world she's trying to escape. But there's a formality in her manner that keeps giving her away.

Absent-mindedly Hannah pushes up the sleeve of her windcheater. Wrapped around her forearm like the imprint of a snake is a deep, purple bruise, a halo of yellow at its edges.

Marcus fixes on it. 'What happened?'

'Colorful, isn't it? I got it from the reel and line at the lifesaving club. The line got tangled.'

'Were you in trouble?'

'I suppose I was. But I was meant to be learning how to use it. I thought it would help me to surf.'

She tells him about the first time she went surfing with Jake, about going over the falls and being pinned down by the wave until she thought her lungs would burst. About scrambling for the surface and wondering if she would ever get there, about longing for the sky. Next time that happens, she says, she wants to know what to do. The lifesavers know about survival and she is determined to learn their secrets.

She leans back and laughs. 'The secrets of staying alive.'

'You're doing it at the lifesaving club?'

Hannah nods, watching him closely.

Marcus feels the smile on his face dissolving. Does she have no idea of what she's done? It doesn't matter to Marcus but he knows how Jake will react. He will seize on it for sure. It's the kind of excuse he always manages to find when anyone looks like getting too close.

'I'm not joining or anything,' she says quickly, as though sensing his unease. 'It's about learning to read the ocean.'

Marcus sips his beer and wonders what hope there can be for them, for her and Jake. Hannah thinks she's preparing herself for the unexpected, that she's taking control of her life. But Marcus knows there will always be events that nothing can prepare you for.

In the teeming rock pools, anemones sink deep into themselves and tiny fish flee into the crevices. For a brief moment the sea holds its breath.

Then the water returns. A wave of colossal size towers

over the dunes. A black wave that dredges up the sunless depths where no life can exist. A wave that arcs so high it drags the sun, stars and moon from the sky and turns the night to pitch. Even the rotunda at the top of the cliff is swamped as thousands of tonnes of water come crashing over the land, ripping low scrub from the sandy earth and collapsing fibro houses like cards as it steams towards the town.

The wave is more than water. It carries a whole universe inside it. What is tossed up from the sea churns with the debris of the land as the inundation gains momentum. Shells, jellyfish, driftwood and deckchairs, bladder-wrack, corrugated iron, car tyres and starfish spiral down the deserted main street as Ruben's goes under, its neon lights still glowing beneath the water.

In the bank, the vault bursts open and the stored wealth of the town turns to instant mush. A siren blares from the fire brigade depot and then gurgles into silence. Mannequins from the drapers crash through the glass windows and bob up cloaked with weed. As the wave engulfs the whole town and finally spends itself in the bay, the only sign of what lies below is the limestone tower of the Continental rising above the surface, its shredded windsock flapping in surrender.

TWELVE

'WHAT HAVE I BEEN doing all night?'

Marie looks at Ruben, wondering how much to say. Does she look tired? Are there grey shadows under her eyes? Or is it simply Ruben's mind? Last night when she rang to say that she couldn't get home, that she was too tired to drive the distance, he seemed to understand. Even if she tells him exactly what she did, he will still think there's more. It's enough that he knows someone was with her at the zoo. Nothing she can say will ease his fears.

'Roo.'

Ruben looks at her sharply. It is a long time since she has called him that.

'Believe me. If it wasn't true I'd come up with a better excuse than a night at the YWCA.'

Ruben keeps polishing the windows. He has been at it all morning. Tidying, cleaning, re-arranging the shelves. The worse things get between them, the more sparkling the cafe becomes. Marie can see that he won't be persuaded. That he needs to believe a third person is to blame for what has happened to them.

'You haven't even noticed,' he says after a long silence.

He points to the far corner of the cafe. A large, rectangular object with a domed top, is covered by a sheet.

'Go on,' he says.

Marie pulls off the sheet. Underneath is a gleaming jukebox like the ones they used to dance to. She reads the list of songs. All hits from the fifties and sixties. She doesn't know what to say.

'It's a handsome machine,' she says finally. 'Practically antique.'

'I thought it might add something.'

'Oh, it does. But the songs—they're not exactly top 40.'

'No.' Ruben's face drops. 'But that's part of the novelty.'

Marie looks at him. She wonders if he believes it himself. He knows the music kids listen to. Angry, raw stuff. Nothing like nostalgia.

'There's another thing too,' he says hurriedly. 'Have a look outside.'

Marie's getting uneasy. She searches the brickwork and windows for clues. It is not until she moves further back into the carpark that she notices a smaller neon sign beneath the one that reads 'Ruben's Cafe'.

'Hold on,' Ruben calls out. 'I'll turn it on.'

The flowing script flickers and then warms up to an orange glow. Four simple words. OPEN ALL NIGHT SATURDAY.

Ruben grins nervously, his head thrust forward like a tortoise coming out of its shell. His balding crown gleams under the late afternoon sun. 'You weren't around. It's a surprise. They're all going across the road but this will bring them back. An all night party. Who else can offer that?'

'You haven't got a licence.'

'That doesn't matter.'

'Why would they come, Ruben, if they can't drink? You didn't tell me. Not a thing.'

Marie had never imagined he would go to these lengths. Ruben was always cautious when it came to the business. He'd thoroughly investigate the options before taking on anything new. It had frustrated her for years, the constant battle for the slightest change.

Ruben watches Marie close her eyes. He can hear the aimless clanking of an aluminium can being blown along in the gutter. He needs her to tell him that he hasn't been a fool, that it was all worth it. But he can't seem to reach her anymore. There's something he remembers from his days of door-to-door. How to communicate with strangers. Find out where the customer is coming from and explain the concept in their terms.

He scrambles for the right phrases. 'Survival of the fittest. Don't compete and you're gone.'

Marie doesn't let him go on. 'Ruben! Please. You don't know what you're saying.' She had no time for Social Darwinism. People who argued like that didn't know the first thing about evolution.

He stops, his face snap-frozen.

'It's crap,' she says wearily, looking up at the sky. She hears herself and winces. She can't bear it when he tries so hard. It only makes things worse.

'Fool,' he says quietly.

Only a few seconds later, after he's gone inside and turned off the sign, does Marie realise that he was talking about himself.

Hannah arrives just before midnight and the place is empty

161

apart from a middle-aged couple leaning over the jukebox, their faces drained by the neon blue tube that illuminates the turn-table. The cafe is dimly lit and seems to be floating in the surrounding darkness as though set adrift at sea. Occasionally, people wander past and peer through the window like curious fish, then quickly turn away toward the blazing lights and laughter across the road.

Hannah has seen this kind of thing before in parts of the city where the restaurants line the streets and people wander, looking for somewhere to eat. There are always a few places that look just like all the others but for some reason people pass them by. Either side the cafes bustle. But in these blighted restaurants, the tables stay empty. Emptiness breeds more emptiness, and crowds attract more crowds and no one ever knows why.

Hannah smiles encouragingly at Ruben who is looking helplessly around the cafe. As always, it is his lot to wait.

'Why's it so dark in here?' she asks.

'Atmosphere.'

Hannah looks out the window at people crossing the road. Ruben follows her eyes.

'They wouldn't know what it is,' he says.

'Go to bed, Ruben. As soon as they close, things will liven up.'

Hannah makes a coffee and wonders what to do with herself until dawn. For a while she stands by the jukebox watching the records drop from their slots and the mechanical arm lowering on to the vinyl. Around one o'clock a smartly dressed group stumble out of the Parlour. They burst through the door of Ruben's like an instant party, and for a moment Hannah wonders if there's hope.

Someone calls out for beer but when they discover that the drinks are soft, the mood immediately sours. One of the men remembers that he has a slab in his boot. 'A slab in your boot, mate?' his friend howls. 'You must have a bloody big foot.' The man is almost out the door when Hannah makes herself heard. The cafe isn't BYO, she tells them. There are groans of disgust. They turn to the jukebox and start drowning out the lyrics with their own. When Hannah goes to the cool room, they leave their food half eaten and disappear without fixing the bill.

By four o'clock the town is dead and Hannah has exhausted the jukebox. Her only customer for the past two hours has been a truck driver with ten dozen Moreton Bay bugs for one of the mansions on the bay.

Hannah sits by the window, like she does on dead afternoons, and rehearses her first 'real' wave. She doesn't lurch to her knees and then topple off, or nose-dive suddenly to take a pounding. She gets it right. Even if the swell is big. Picking off the largest wave she rides it like a magic carpet, performing the kind of manoeuvres that take years to command. Having ridden it for what it's worth, she flicks elegantly off the lip.

In a daze the next morning she watches the sky turn pink above the scrub-covered sandhills at the end of the Ocean Beach Road. She can tell from the stillness and the singed smell of the coming heat that the conditions will be perfect. Already the cicadas have started their aching chant. From out the back of the cafe, Marie is peering over the saloon doors, her face still puffy from sleep, asking how it went. Hannah opens the till. Marie takes one look and sighs.

'You might as well go,' she says.

When Hannah gets to the Long Beach it's practically deserted except for a few fishermen. In the still morning air the ocean wrinkles like the skin of a sleeping dragon. The surf is small and at first it looks as though she is wasting her time. Wave after wave passes beneath her, breaking too close to the shore or not at all. She wonders if she will ever catch a fully formed wave instead of shorebreak mush or the soft shoulder of an already broken peak.

She remembers the frustration of learning to play tennis when she was about ten years old. The lessons were on the asphalt courts nextdoor to her father's red brick church. Out of all the shots she had to learn, she found serving the hardest. She knew there was more to it than swatting her arm and lobbing the ball over the net but couldn't work out what it was. One day she tossed the ball a little higher than usual and came down on top of it, hard. As the ball left the racket she knew she had it. The sound was right. The trick was to throw her whole body behind it like taking a forward dive into space or trying to spear herself into the service court.

The trick was not to hold back. Every bit of energy and judgement had to be put into that moment.

Hannah is thinking about the satisfaction of that serve when she turns around to see a good set rising out of nowhere. This is what she loves and fears the most—the way an ocean desert can suddenly become the Alps.

She paddles toward the line-up, her whole body buzzing. Diamonds glitter on the water and everything is clear-cut. She swings around to position herself, gliding through the surface with clean, rhythmic strokes. Suddenly the wave catches up and a shocking surge of energy lifts her high above the hollowing water. Foam licks at her ankles as the nose of her board dives forward. Like an elevator dropping she is over the edge and skidding down the shoulder, her knees loosening as she rises to her feet. The speed of it is totally unexpected. Her arms fly out like a baby afraid it's about to be dropped. Instinctively she lowers her centre of gravity, bringing herself closer to the wave so that she is almost part of it, no longer just on the surface.

From below comes a deepening rumble, a drawn-out explosion of water meeting the earth's resistance. The wave slows, its energy dissipating. She has ridden it to the brink and it's too late to pull back, even if she could. Something is unfurling inside her, giving itself up to the wave. She is finally letting go.

This is no magic carpet ride. No game of tennis. This is something else altogether.

Marcus sits in the ute, absorbed in the sight of Hannah as she walks up the jetty to where the ferry has docked. She is wearing the halter-neck dress that his son had given her. The cars have started rolling off, but Jake's Holden isn't yet in view.

He watches as she stops halfway. She stands at the very edge, studying the water below. A pelican, which was perched on a nearby rowboat, is slowly unfolding its wings. She turns to Marcus, pointing at the big-beaked bird gracefully taking flight. Her hand rises above her head, revealing the brown hairs of her armpit. The sight of it jolts him. That darkened hollow normally hidden from view. As if she's exposed herself to him, as if she were standing there naked and letting him feast on the view. He drags his eyes away and something lurches inside. He can't go on ignoring what's in his mind.

Something felt not seen. A quiver that travels up through the feet. The trace of an invisible force racing across the ocean.

Jake's car becomes visible and makes its way slowly down the ramp. As it crawls toward them the passenger door flies open. Jake staggers out as if drunk or stoned. He totters across the wooden boards towards Hannah and they fall into a rough embrace, almost toppling into the water. Straining to hold Jake up, Hannah motions over his shoulder for Marcus to come and help.

In the front seat of the ute, Hannah sits between father and son, Jake slumped on her shoulder. Marcus feels the warmth of her thigh when they turn a corner and she slides his way. He focuses on the road ahead, occasionally glancing at Jake. He wonders if his son has finally pushed himself too far.

At the house they carry Jake inside and put him to bed. A doctor is called. Jake has a bad viral infection, but the worst is over. When Marcus checks on him later, the sheets are bunched at the end of the bed. The mattress is soaked with sweat.

Over the next few days Hannah and Marcus do shifts at his bedside while Jake thrashes, delirious. Now and then

Marcus's face will appear above him. He smiles and touches his forehead, presses something wet to his lips. Sometimes, it's Hannah but she always seems a long way off. Sometimes no one is there and he sinks below to that deep-sea world of fish with neon entrails, glowing gills, and jaws like aliens. A dark world full of strange booms and grunts, clicks and high-pitched chatter. Sometimes when both Hannah and Marcus are there, he sees them whispering to each other, and he's sure they're plotting against him.

Hannah comes straight from work to give Marcus a break. They sit in the kitchen and talk over cups of coffee about Jake. Then Hannah insists that Marcus get some rest.

Lying in bed he can hear her moving backwards and forwards between Jake's room and the kitchen. Sometimes she passes his door to go to the bathroom. He hears the shower go on, the sound of the water hitting the tiles and the changing rhythm when she steps naked beneath it.

The week passes and Jake sleeps more heavily. He doesn't twitch or shift or mutter any more. He lies on his back with his mouth open and arms flung out, his hair spread on the pillow like he's floating in a pool. Marcus is encouraged by his peacefulness but there's something about the way Jake looks that still disturbs him.

Gradually the fever drops. Jake is soon noticing the weather. By the end of the week he's talking to Hannah about going for a surf. From the kitchen, Marcus can hear their conversation.

'You're crazy,' Hannah tells him.

'And you're mad,' he says.

'Why mad?'

'With me. For going.'

'Not any more.'

'That's good,' he laughs, patting the mattress. 'Come here.'

The door closes. Marcus decides it's time for the shopping. It's enough to know Jake's better. There are some things he'd rather not hear.

The heat has sapped their energy. Hannah kneels between his outstretched legs and buries her head in his groin. Jake fingers her lazily as he slips in and out of sleep. She would like to ask him what happened while he was away. She can see he's been through an ordeal. Everything about him is frayed. There's a nasty gash on his forehead, the skin on his nose is raw, and his eyebrows and lashes are no longer gold but white.

There's so much Hannah wants to find out, but she knows better now than to ask. No point trying to drag it out of him. Jake's still too close to the edge. She'll have to stay in the dark a bit longer. Let him tell her in his own time. But how much time have they got? Perhaps it's only at moments like this, with the door closed on the world, that they'll ever make it work.

They doze for hours in the stifling room until Hannah stirs and opens a window. Her mouth is parched. They get up dazed and sticky; take a shower and raid the fridge. Jake has that worn, hungry look he gets after late nights. He leans on the door frame then traps her against the wall, pressing himself to her. Laughing with exhaustion, they clutch at one another as they sink on to the floor. Neither has the energy to move.

When Marcus gets back, he finds them in the hallway, crouched in each others arms.

The next day when Hannah arrives after work, Jake is dressed and wandering restlessly around the house.

'Cabin fever,' he tells her. 'I gotta get out for a surf.'

When they pull into the Long Beach, Hannah is relieved that no one else is around. As she paddles out there's a smoothness and confidence in her action that Jake can't help but notice. She launches herself on the first good wave that comes her way and quickly finds her feet. Jake detours to clear her path, whooping as she passes. When the fluid shelf folds in on itself, Hannah dives sideways and comes up gasping. Jake is doing a tap dance on his board. He scoops across the water toward her, still hooting with delight. He tells her he can't believe it. How far she's come while he's been away.

Looking pleased with himself he adds, 'I'd say you had a good teacher.'

Hannah avoids his eyes. She will tell him about the lifesaving later. When the moment is right.

They surf until the sun has bled itself into the sea and the swell has died away. Hannah straddles her board, savoring the dying light. She is the happiest she's been all summer. She wishes she knew how to make it last. Soon Jake is just a silhouette and the occasional flash of white teeth. It becomes too dark to see and they paddle to shore, disappearing into the dunes. When they emerge, they're covered in an armour of tiny scales from rolling in the sand.

In the carpark they are brushing each other down when

a car comes over the hill and they are caught like night animals in the high beam. The lights flash at them and Hannah screens her eyes, trying to make out who it is. The car pulls up alongside them and a woman's head pops out of the front window.

'Hannah honey!'

She can't see the woman's face, but she's known that crackling voice since primary school. Tessa. Someone she wouldn't call a friend, even though they grew up in the same street.

Tessa is bubbling with exclamations and laughter. Once over her initial surprise, Hannah slips into conversation while Jake stands silently nearby. He doesn't warm to this flouncy thing and he doesn't like the way she looks at him. He watches Hannah, the change in her manner, the knowing, worldly tone of her voice. They are talking about some university lecturer. What he gets up to.

Jake looks around restlessly. He is getting cold and the surf has knocked him about. Perhaps more than he thought. That manic, high-pitched chatter is still fresh in his mind. He flexes his fingers, trying to make a fist but he hasn't got the strength. Hannah reckoned she was sick of uni and now she is talking about it like it's the most fantastic thing in the world. It's too much for Jake.

'So he fucks his students? Big deal.'

'Who said it was?' Hannah's face tightens.

Tessa is eying Jake. 'Anyway, hon. Got to go. Be seeing you.'

She drives off with a toot of her horn. Hannah turns to Jake who is trying to look sorry.

'She was giving me the shits.' He runs his hands across her shoulders and down her arms.

Hannah starts to pull away.

Jake holds her there. 'C'mon, don't be like that. Let's go back. I'll be your lecturer. You tell me what he does.'

Hannah sleeps more soundly than she has in weeks. She wakes to find Jake still out to it and the late morning sun slicing through the venetians. She lies on her back enjoying the warmth of his body and the memory of yesterday's surf. She stretches out, her muscles aching, pleasantly. She's thinking about getting up for work when she hears footsteps on the front path and then a knock at the door. She waits, hoping the caller will go. But after a long pause there's another louder and more insistent knock.

Hannah gets up slowly. Pulls on the nearest thing she can find, one of Jake's t-shirts with a surfing rat on the front. She opens the door and immediately wishes she hadn't. Anton is standing on the porch smiling, like he's about to arrest her or something. She's conscious of her bare legs and of the sticky sleep in the corners of her eyes.

'Feeling fit?' he asks.

'Fit enough.'

He flicks his eyes over her body.

'I reckon you would be. All that training. So how's the beach police. Been on patrol yet?' He pauses for effect. 'What's Jake think?'

Hannah has one hand on the door and Anton is still on the doorstep. She could easily slam it and buy some time. She's said nothing to Jake. She was afraid he wouldn't understand. Even though she'd finished at the club two weeks before.

Hannah had always thought that Anton's cool, provocative manner was just a pose, a way of protecting himself. But now she sees there's more to it than that. He's come to stir up trouble.

'I haven't mentioned it. What's it to you?'

Anton shrugs. 'It's your bed.' He steps past her and into the hall. 'How's the boy?'

'Asleep.'

Hannah has just finished speaking when Jake calls out, asking who's there.

'Not any more,' Anton says as he heads to the bedroom.

THIRTEEN

AUSTRALIA DAY ARRIVES AND with it a highway choked with cars heading south for one last fling before the working year begins. Jake pulls up at the Long Beach to find all the carparks full. The attendant tells him he will have to go elsewhere. Jake stares out the window in disgust.

Families loaded up with towels, surf mats and eskies file past his car as they make their way down the cliff. The children lag behind, moaning about the distance and the weight of their loads. The parents ignore their protests, shouting at them to hurry up. For a moment Jake contemplates driving straight through the boom gates and mowing into the crowd, just to see them squeal. Instead, he lets his tyres screech as he does a u-turn and speeds back along the road to the Sphinx. From there he walks up the beach toward the club house.

It's a muggy afternoon. The air charged and sparky. A storm is on the way. 'Good Vibrations' is playing on the public address system as dark clouds come hulking in from the west. The surf is starting to chop when Jake notices Hannah heading out towards him. He hasn't seen her for days, not since Anton came around. She had slipped off to work without saying goodbye. She draws up beside him and dives her hand under the water, making a playful grab for his toes. He pulls away and his foot jerks up, just missing her eye. Water sprays in her face. She looks at him warily.

'You've got sensitive toes.'

'Leave them alone.'

Before any more can be said, an approaching set leaves them scrambling. Jake paddles for the wave as if Hannah wasn't there. He has just caught it when he glances over his shoulder to see her right behind him, shooting out of the clouds and skidding across the wave he's on. She's smiling as if nothing was wrong, as if the world was her oyster, as if everything was as it should be. There's wave enough for them both, a chance for a double act, but Jake digs in and clumsily swerves away. He flicks off the lip and Hannah takes it all the way to the beach.

The light has turned a lurid yellow. The music is cut and a voice booms out a warning to the surfers who have strayed between the flags. It had been happening a lot that summer—the best break on the beach being made out of bounds. The surfers tried to stay out the back and keep away from the swimmers but inevitably someone would lose it and swerve into the crowd. Sure enough the rubber dinghy would come powering over the whitewater to herd the surfers off.

Most of them drift reluctantly away, protesting loudly, until Jake is the only one left. Turning to face the club house he raises a finger and paddles back to the line-up. Any other year Jake might've just let it be and moved on to Sphinx or London Bridge, knowing that the season was about to end and that soon the beach would be his. But things have gone too far.

He sits on his board punching the water and turning

over in his mind what Anton told him. Louie had seen
Hannah with the clubbies, doing training exercises and
rescue drills. At the edge, where the sand was dark and
sodden, they practised mouth to mouth. A group of them
went running along the beach, did push-ups on the sand
and thumped over the waves in the club's rubber boat.
The image of it made Jake sick. With each succeeding
year, it was not only his territory the clubbies invaded,
but his head as well. He hated the way they came down
on weekends and told the locals how to behave. He hated
their self-righteousness and all that bronzed Aussie shit.
Most of all, he hated the way they set themselves up as
the law.

In the past he'd made a policy of keeping his distance
from anyone who came from the city. Especially since that
girl at the Quinceys. He saw the way they behaved on
their holidays and the mess they left behind. They could
always pick up and go back to their other lives. But for
the locals there was nowhere else.

Then Hannah had come along and taken him by
surprise. Jake knew they were an unlikely pair. When she
started talking about poetry, he remembered something
from *Hamlet*—'Alas poor Yorick'—but he couldn't think of
the rest. Sometimes he'd sing along with Elvis Costello and
make it clear the words were for her. This was the poetry
he liked. He was good at 'crooning'. He could tell from
the way she leaned back in the seat and looked at him
sidelong, that she liked it too.

Lately, things had started to work in a wordless way.
He hadn't thought about it too much because in the past
that had led to trouble. He'd get restless or scared and

want out. Now he was angry. Angry that she hadn't even told him. That she'd tried to fool him, keep him thinking he'd been the one who'd taught her. Just like Anton had taught him.

Anton said it only confirmed what he'd always suspected. She'd gone back to where she belonged.

Hannah is contending with the shorebreak when she sees Jake paddling between the flags. Another warning booms from the loudspeakers and everyone on the beach is looking in his direction. She sees his finger go up and hears jeers from the club house. From a group of lifesavers in a huddle, Fraser emerges and comes bounding across the sand. Hannah stands in the waist-deep water, her board floating at her side. Fraser wades out toward her, his jaw set hard like a cop.

'That friend of yours, Hannah. Do him a favor. Get him out of the way or we'll do it for you.'

Hannah scowls and barely nods. The soft-faced boy is showing his other side. She doesn't want to be their messenger but Jake will pay if she refuses.

They will confiscate his board, Fraser adds, and make him kiss their arses to get it back.

Hannah paddles out, her arms stiff and heavy. Jake is sitting on his board with his back to the beach, hunched over like the whole world is against him. His hair is plastered to his head and neck, and from behind he looks even wirier than usual. All the others have moved away. Big drops of rain are starting to pit the surface of the water.

'Jake,' she calls as soon as she is close enough. He doesn't move and she calls again. She's almost reached him when he swivels around sharply. He looks at her darkly and tells her to go back to her friends.

'They're not my friends.'

'Bullshit.'

She forces herself to say it. 'If you don't move they'll take your board.'

'Thanks for the advice. Go tell them where to shove it.'

'Jake. Please. They'll be gone tomorrow. We'll have it to ourselves then.'

'Ourselves?'

Hannah closes her eyes. This is no place for a fight and no time, either.

'Let's go in, Jake. We can talk about it there.'

Another set is coming through, its neat corrugations steadily advancing.

'Give up,' he throws over his shoulder as he paddles out to meet it.

Hannah is back on the beach stripping off her wetsuit when the boat goes out. To get past the breaking waves it has to make a detour through the rip and as it does, Jake slips away and catches a wave to shore. Hannah watches him emerge from the foam, yank his leg rope off and sling it over the board. There is no point trying to talk to him now, not with Anton and the others around.

Down near the tide line Jake is deep in discussion with Anton, Louie and Mitch. They stand kicking at the sand, sometimes glancing at the club house. Other surfers are wandering across to join them. Soon there is quite a group. Watching them together, Hannah wonders how she ever imagined they'd accept her as one of them.

Confronting Jake has left her numbed. She doesn't want

to think about it. She tells herself they'll sort it out like they've always done—in bed. They can't seem to help themselves. But for now all she can do is watch. She moves further up the beach, spreads out her towel and waits. The air is fresher. The storm is passing over like a travelling show just off shore, leaving the bathers untouched. Its great puffs of grey and white send out flashes of light and trail a haze of rain. As the yellow bruised cloud withdraws to the east, everybody turns to the gathering on the beach.

It is four in the morning when Ruben wakes and finds the bed empty. He brushes his hand over the space. It's still warm. There's the click of a switch and a strip of light cuts across the hallway. He hears the toilet flush, water in the basin and then, after a long pause, the loungeroom door opens and feet pad across the carpet. He imagines her standing at the window looking out over the old highway. He can see her outline from behind, her body wrapped in her summer dressing-gown that always hangs alongside his on the back of the door. He imagines himself standing behind her and gently drawing it from her shoulders. He kisses each sunburnt mound, runs his lips across the nape of her neck and feels her shiver. Her dressing-gown falls to her feet and he places his arms gently around her.

Suddenly the saloon doors snap and the image dissolves. She slips through his grasp and into the shop. After that there is silence. He can't follow her now. It's as if she's stepped into absolute darkness, to a place where his mind can't go. When he was a child he used to try to imagine 'forever'. It made his head ache to do it. But still he'd push through outer space, past solar system after solar system, out into the depths of the universe until he couldn't bear it any more. He kept waiting for the end, of time and place. But it never came. Trailing her now was like that. It hurt too much; he had fallen too far behind.

He has to get up for the milk delivery soon. He is aching to sleep but his mind is sharp and bleak. Usually, at this time of year, he's looking forward to the end of the season. Enough money has been made to carry them through the winter and the long hours are beginning to tell. When the mad rush is over everything can return to the familiar routines. More time for billiards and cards, for reading the paper and doing the cryptic. More time to sleep and think. More energy for all those things that have gone neglected over the summer.

But this year he doesn't want it to end. When the madness is over and the people go home, everything will fall apart. There will be nothing but a dark stretch of time unravelling before him. He no longer thinks 'if she goes' but 'when she goes'. And when she goes all the familiar routines will lose their power to reassure. The endless chores, the daily small talk, the view out the window, the smell of the food. He cannot imagine enduring it alone.

He dozes, then starts and dozes again until the watery light of day begins to seep through the blinds. He feels her body sink into the bed like a deep sigh. Soon she is breathing the light, rhythmic breath of sleep.

Ruben is locking up when Marie pulls into the carpark late that afternoon. She rattles the door handle and reaches for her keys before realising that Ruben is on the other side. Through the glass she smiles brightly at him, the kind of smile that signals bad news. The kind of smile nurses wear to cheer up a dying patient. She glances at him quickly and then disappears out the back of the shop.

Ruben is circling the billiard table. Marie can see him through the open door, his long body arched over the polished wood. In the first few years of their marriage she had loved his lankiness and his soulful face. She'd also loved his restraint. He was never casual with his touch and all physical contact seemed especially charged. It was something to be savored. But over the years she'd lost interest. The charge had gone. A starved, hollow look has crept into his features and all she can feel is pity.

Ruben puts his cue back in the upright holder and leans on the table.

'Well then,' he says.

Marie steps out of the doorway and into the garage. She looks across at the scoreboard with its row of numbers and moveable pointers like the beads of an abacas. She is forty-six, Ruben is fifty. They have been married for twenty-nine years. What is the sum of those years together? What does it amount to? The figures are meaningless.

She tells him she has been to see the solicitor. He has drawn up the papers. She will stay for as long as it takes to sort things out. She asks him what he wants to do about the cafe. He asks her how she will support herself. They stand at opposite ends of the table. In flat, far-away voices they talk about the dissolution of their marriage.

FOURTEEN

HANNAH SITS IN THE dark. Outside the loungeroom window the street lights make the road look wet. As the wind shuffles through the trees there's the sound of water falling. Like a downpour that will never cease. For hours she has been watching the puffy heads of the hydrangeas bob against the front fence. In her hand there's an apple. She took a bite from it over an hour ago.

At midnight she gets up from the armchair and pulls down the blinds. She walks around the room negotiating the grey shapes in her path.

He's not coming. She's known it for ages but as long as cars kept turning into the street there had been hope. She moves through the house not bothering to switch on the lights.

She has to get out.

At first she just walks, taking the back streets. She tries to keep her mind blank but the thoughts keep pressing in on her, like the crowds at the Long Beach as they gathered when the fight broke out. It'd been funny at first. Somehow Louie got inside the club house and before anyone realised, he'd replaced the Beach Boys with the Sex Pistols and turned the volume up full. The gravelly voice of Johnny Rotten singing 'God Save the Queen' exploded over the beach. Louie came hurtling out with three lifesavers in pursuit and made a dash for the safety of the group.

It might have ended there. She couldn't tell who made the first move. There were shouts from both sides as sand and bodies began flying. More lifesavers came running from the club house as though descending from the sky, their caps flapping like miniature parachutes as they ran. After that, it was useless.

The house is in darkness when she presses the bell. Stepping back into the garden she looks up to see a light go on in the hallway. Marcus opens the door and ushers her in. He is wearing an old-fashioned tweed dressing-gown with wide lapels and a tassel around the waist. His feet are bare.

They sit in the back room. It is a part of the house she has never been in, a world away from the plain, suburban facade. With the blue glow of the television for light, they might be in a museum under the sea. Glass-fronted cabinets filled with shells and other objects line three walls. On the mantelpiece are more shells, large ones with beautiful swirls, wide open mouths and beckoning orange interiors. In the tilted mirror behind, Hannah sees herself sitting next to Marcus, his hair rumpled and his face creased.

'I've woken you up,' she says, wishing she hadn't come. She has run to the father in search of the son.

'Not at all. I've been watching the box.'

Hannah continues as though Marcus hadn't spoken. 'I didn't think about what I was doing. I started walking and ended up here.' She puts down her coffee. 'I better go.'

'Not on your own you're not.'

'The dark doesn't worry me.'

'It worries me. It worries me to think of you out there on your own. Where's Jake?'

'I haven't seen him for days.'

Almost a month ago, they'd planned to celebrate Hannah's birthday at the Fish House restaurant in town. Even after days of silence, she'd refused to believe he wouldn't show.

'You thought he might be with me?'

'Not really.'

'I'm flattered you came. You're always welcome here. At any hour.'

Hannah meets his eyes and she might be staring at Jake. As they talk she sees flashes of him that are gone before she can pin them down. Like an afterglow, they register more in her body than her eye.

'He's living with Anton now.'

Hannah nods. She had heard from Sam. The boys were still friendly enough in a distant way. At least they came to the cafe. She could understand that they didn't want to get involved. What'd happened had only confirmed their suspicions that she didn't fit into their scheme of things. She was a tourist like all the rest.

'Suddenly I don't exist,' Hannah says.

Marcus laces his fingers together and makes a soothing sound deep in his throat.

'Jake doesn't mean to hurt you. He gets wild sometimes. It's just the way he is.'

Hannah says she's not surprised after what happened. It all went so badly wrong.

Marcus fingers a brown cowry shell as though it were a worry bead. He looks down at the polished floorboards and shakes his head. 'If it hadn't been the clubbies, he would've found another reason.'

'To break it off?'

'Put it this way, Hannah. He has trouble keeping things going.'

'But why?'

'Who knows,' Marcus says, not wanting to go on with it. 'You do what you can but sometimes it isn't enough.'

Hannah waits for him to explain. After a long pause Marcus looks up apologetically. There's something withdrawn about him now and she feels responsible.

She looks around at his collection. The cabinets are stacked like bookshelves, one on top of the other, halfway up each wall. In the far corner is a small wooden stepladder. As well as the shells, she can see jars with small creatures floating in them, their dimensions warped by the glass. There are also bits of bone, teeth and tiny skulls bleached by the sun; coral and sponge, seahorses and sunstars; the dried and lacquered bodies of puffed-out fish and the x-ray images of fossils in rock. One cabinet is full of human relics, ordinary objects of mysterious provenance transformed by the ocean—wood from wrecked vessels or lost cargo, bottles and glass, a brass compass partially encrusted, and something oval like a glass eye.

Hannah moves from cabinet to cabinet. Here is an obsession of a different kind. Souvenirs and *memento mori*. An obsession with absence. When she first arrived she was bursting with questions that might conjure up Jake, make sense of what had happened and help her understand. She could think of nothing else. But now the need is less urgent. The room itself is full of answers.

Standing at her side, Marcus tells the story behind each object and the method of preservation used. He has friends among the fishermen who bring him shells from the stomachs of the fish they catch. Some of his best specimens have been found this way. He discusses other techniques of collecting and the tools of his trade. To Hannah, the details are curious and seemingly random. He confides his aversion to the use of forceps, so often used to prise the animals out of their shells or off the rocks. Forceps, he believes, should be the tools of delivery, of birth, not death.

Rarity, in either scientific or collectors' terms, does not seem to interest him. Each object has a significance determined by some personal code of value that Hannah cannot quite fathom. From the last cabinet he removes a small piece of white, ribbed shell and places it in her hand.

'This is a fragment of the paper nautilus,' he says cryptically, then returns it to the shelf.

The tour over, he points to a book open on the table. There's a glossy photograph of a series of shells from the families Nautilidae and Argonautidae. Some are pearly and smooth with tiger stripes, others are snowy white and covered in tiny ridges and peaks. They have that classic look of objects which have been symbols for so long it surprises her to find that they are real. Even more surprising is the sketch, on the opposite page, of the creature which made them.

'An octopus?'

Marcus smiles and nods.

Hannah thinks of the Back Beach at low tide, of the deep pools that harbor octopuses and giant crabs. As a young girl she and her friends would taunt them with nets filled with starfish and other bait they could find. The tentacles of the octopus would get tangled in the net and she could lift it clear of the water and watch it writhe. Glistening suckers gulped at the air, threatening to drag her down into its watery world. Then one time she noticed an eye at the base of the bulbous head, and its inner life glimmered at her. The game was up. All the exquisite terror fell away. It was no longer a mythical beast but a living creature in torment. She threw it back.

'We forget the creature that makes the shell,' he is saying with a fervor Hannah has not detected before. He speaks of how the paper nautilus is formed, and how the young force the female from the shell once they hatch; how the male is a fraction the size of his partner and was once thought to be a parasite in the female's shell. With some indignation, he tells her how scientists call it a pseudo shell because it's secreted for incubating rather than inhabiting. Then suddenly weary of his own voice, he stops mid-explanation and gently closes the book, as though finishing a bedtime story.

Hannah gets up to go but Marcus won't hear of it.

'You can stay in Jake's old room,' he says.

Marcus smiles at her. He knows she won't be able to resist the invitation. He watches her go and wishes he could follow.

~~

Hannah walks along the highway with her back to the traffic. She sticks out a thumb and prays that a woman will pick her up. Until a few days ago she had never hitched before. The hike to the beach is a long one with a board in tow, and the buses run every three hours. All the time she is listening for the sound of Jake's car. She only sees him from a distance now. Sometimes she catches sight of him in the township, sometimes at the beach. Sometimes she sees him driving past the cafe, but he never stops. If Ruben or Marie have noticed that Jake is not around any more, they haven't said. They have other things on their minds.

Whenever Hannah sees a blond shock of hair sitting near the aspidistra her heart starts to thump, but she is always disappointed. Sometimes she sees him with Anton or the boys, sometimes he is alone. So far, she hasn't seen him with another woman. She has become adept at finding signs of repressed desire in even his coldest gestures. He ignores her because he's afraid his resolve will weaken. He refuses to speak to her because his voice might betray his feelings.

She can hear wheels on the gravel. Hannah steels herself and turns around. She bends to the window and peers inside knowing she's playing Russian roulette. Sometimes she can hardly believe that she's doing it. So far she has been lucky. So far the threats have come to nothing. The fat man in the mini minor asked if he could touch her breast. But it was more a wistful request than a proposition and he didn't protest when she demanded to be let out. The duckshooter in the four wheel drive gave her more of a scare. He was casually confiding how much he liked 'shootin' things dead' when she noticed his rifle propped up in the back.

There's something about this driver that she doesn't like, the way his eyes slide all over her, his eagerness for her to get in. 'No thanks,' she says, slamming the door and stepping back as he accelerates away. Hannah watches him disappear down the highway and wonders where the ride might have led. There's a fire hydrant up ahead. She leans her board against it and sits on the flat, red top. She closes her eyes. The daily trip to the beach has become an ordeal, a test of will. And she's determined not to give in.

A car blasts its horn and speeds by. Her eyes snap open. She hates the way people check her out with no intention of stopping. She's mustering the energy to get up when she hears the deep animal roar of a semi-trailer changing gears as it slows. It looks like the icecream truck that makes deliveries to Ruben's. She can't pick the driver's face but he's wearing a company uniform. He throws her board in the freezer with the cartons of Drumsticks and Choc Wedges while she climbs into the cabin. He's friendly enough and the talk is relaxed as they power their way to the beach. As she looks down on the cars below, she's starting to think that maybe she can handle this, that maybe it isn't so bad. It's just a matter of picking your lifts.

Her board is slightly frosted when he hands it back.

'Like a stiff,' he jokes as he the closes the doors of the freezer. Back in the driver's seat he leans out the window. His smile is gone. 'You were mad to ride with me. That could've been you in the back.' He drives off in a cloud of sand and exhaust.

That evening it's Marcus who pulls up beside her. Hannah doesn't care that he's angry. She almost cries with relief.

'I thought you had more sense,' he says with real disappointment. She must have known he'd be happy to drive her. 'All you had to do was ask.'

'I didn't want to bother you. I wanted to get around by myself.'

Marcus is getting agitated just thinking about what might have happened. She seems to have lost sight of the difference between being foolhardy and being brave. He's seen the same bloody-mindedness in Jake. He pulls the car over to the side of the road and cuts the engine, then reaches out his sun-scarred arms and takes her by the shoulders.

'Look,' he says. 'I don't know what you're trying to prove. But you're asking for trouble. There are madmen out there just waiting.'

He doesn't want to alarm her but he has to make her see the risk she's running. Instead his urgency communicates something he hadn't intended.

Hannah is looking at him, her eyes slightly closed. A clinical, inquiring gaze. She's studying his face as though she can't quite make up her mind.

'I was just trying to get to the beach.'

Marcus removes his hands from her shoulders and glances in the rear vision mirror. He'll have to watch himself. If he's not careful, he'll only make things worse.

In the days that follow, Marcus drives Hannah to the surf and takes her home in the evenings. They've just arrived at the Long Beach carpark one morning when Hannah sees Jake's Holden coming over the hill. Marcus is leaning against the cabin of the Dodge and doesn't notice Jake's arrival. Hannah keeps on talking as though nothing has happened. She's pulling her wetsuit over her bathers and fumbling around her back for the zip. Knowing that Jake will have seen them, she asks Marcus to do her up.

As she turns back to him, she moves one step closer. Suddenly they're face to face. For a moment she pauses there. They're breathing each other's breath. She bends forward and gives him a slow kiss on the lips.

'That's for looking after me,' she says.

Over Marcus's head, Hannah can see Jake staring at them with a look of disbelief. Stung into life, he swings the Holden around and presses his foot down hard. Revving the engine furiously, he roars back over the hill.

Marcus works at his bench chipping at a rusted lump of metal thick with barnacles. Nearby Hannah stands watching. She knows she must stop seeing him. It's a dangerous game she's playing but she doesn't know how to stop. Now Jake refuses to speak to his father and Marcus has no idea why. Each day she's determined to come clean with him, but something always holds her back.

Everything is falling apart. Marie has finally made the break and spends most of her time in the city. The cafe is up for sale and Ruben has retreated so far into himself that no one can reach him. The question of what to do with the year ahead is looming ever larger, and Hannah has no one but Marcus to talk to. And she knows that he wants her company as much as she needs his.

Hannah wanders around the work room. On the mantelpiece, behind the massive conch, she discovers a framed photograph. A family shot of Marcus, Jake and his mother, Ellen. Hannah examines each parent closely trying to piece Jake together. His mother stands slightly taller than his father and draws the viewer's eye with her high cheekbones and bold stare. The edges of her dress are blurred, perhaps stirred by the wind or by her own movement. Her mouth is partly open as if she's about to speak. Hannah can almost hear her voice. She's young and impatient and full of life. Her hand rests on her young son's head and he's grabbing hold of her leg, afraid she might get away.

Hannah stares at Ellen for a long time, waiting for her to step out of the frame. She knows that restless energy so well it almost hurts to look at her. It's hard to believe that someone so defiantly alive could suddenly cease to be. Jake had always refused to talk about her. Sometimes Marcus seems on the verge of it. But he always stops short and changes the subject.

Only when Hannah watches him at work on his collection, does she begin to understand the sadness and longing in him. It's there in the way he holds the shells; the way he touches their smooth insides and tapering lips; the way he chants their Latin names; the way he polishes them with oil and holds them up to the light.

He takes a rectangular-shaped bivalve from the shelf, runs his fingers cautiously along its edges and asks her opinion.

'What would you name it?'

Hannah studies it and shrugs. She has no idea.

'The common name is a razor shell. The old-fashioned cut-throat variety.' He holds it up to his cheek as though about to shave. 'But the Latin name, that's something else. *Solen vaginoides.*'

With a private smile he explains. Early collectors had been reluctant to adopt the Linnaean system of classification—genus and species—because of its allusions to parts of the female anatomy. In the eighteenth century, the resemblances which Linnaeus saw made people uneasy. Collectors would have to label their shells with these names, or worse, utter them in discussions with their peers.

Marcus puts the shell back on the shelf. 'Perhaps it told them something about themselves they didn't want to know. Shell collecting was supposed to be a recreation for gentlemen. What they thought was a hobby turned out to be more than it seemed.'

Marcus reaches for another shell—dull in color on the outside, but with a glossy, fluted opening. 'Look at this. Spengler's rock whelk. Or this, Roadnight's volute. The names don't matter. You can see the likeness for yourself.'

Hannah is starting to feel out of her depth. That familiar warning voice is sounding in her head.

You should not be here.

FIFTEEN

Ruben has gone off his game and the table has remained untouched for over a month. Everything is too much of an effort. Even the balls seem to move in slow motion across the baize. Unable to play to form, he has lost the desire to play at all. The last game he played he gave up in disgust. Instead of covering the table as he usually did with the plastic sheets and wooden slats, he threw an old blanket over it and locked the garage door behind him.

Then the woman who bought the cafe came for the final inspection and insisted on looking the table over. When Ruben pulled back the blanket, he could have cried. The silverfish had been feasting. All across the baize there were large, ragged spaces with the grey slate showing through. The eaten parts looked like continents surrounded by a green sea. A map of the world spread out before them but it wasn't the world that Ruben knew.

February is over. The town grows quiet as the university students stagger back to the city, always the last to leave. From a toenail slither, the moon grows steadily until one night it emerges full blown from behind the clouds. People arriving at Ruben's and Marie's farewell pause outside the cafe and point to the giant yellow globe that seems to be resting on the earth.

To enter the cafe they must pass the floodlit FOR SALE sign that boasts of a 'thriving seaside business in a relaxed setting offering unlimited rewards to the industrious'. No one pauses to read the finer print. A bold black and green SOLD sign is plastered across the board. Speaking in low voices the guests move quickly inside, unsure how to behave. The occasion is the sale, but everyone knows. It might as well be a wake for Marie's and Ruben's marriage.

The turnout is big and the cafe quickly fills. The tables and benches have been pushed to the walls to make space for dancing. Ruben is serving beer and cocktails from behind one counter which he has transformed into a bar. There are colorful, intoxicating milkshakes and mixed drinks garnished with summer umbrellas and cherries on toothpicks, slices of lime and stuffed olives. The walls are decorated with streamers and balloons that slowly shrink as the night wears on.

Friends and acquaintances shake Ruben's hand, wish him well and tell him he will be missed. Nobody seems to know what more to say, and Ruben can't really blame them. People know how to celebrate marriages or mourn at funerals, but there's no protocol for an occasion like this. It was his idea to hold the party. Marie had wanted nothing to do with it. She was afraid it was a final, desperate ploy to make her change her mind.

Although he's not religious Ruben has always found ceremony comforting. His own set of rituals in the cafe— the ones that so infuriated Marie—gave his work a kind of meaning beyond the mundane actions themselves. At the end of every day he'd run through his list of tasks and only when they were completed could he start to relax. He needed to finish things properly, to formally observe the end.

And yet as he watches Marie moving among their guests, responding brightly to the forced smiles and treading cautiously between camps, he knows it isn't that simple. He's not capable of an explosion, of venting his anger that way. But if he doesn't do something with it, he's in danger of going mad. With every trip to the city, Marie had been making a new life while Ruben went on as before. When it suited her, the marriage was over. She wanted to slip quietly away, to disappear for good. But he couldn't let that happen. He had to make her face up to what she'd done.

Occasionally someone will offer to take Ruben's place behind the bar so that he can join the party. 'Later,' he tells them as he pours another beer and hands it over. He's happy to stay where he is and watch the whole thing unfold. His legs are growing tired and his feet are beginning to ache. He leans against the counter until it's the only thing keeping him up.

Marie clutches a plate of sausage rolls and pizza wedges thick with topping. She senses wariness all around her.

'Ruben got a good price,' says Beatrice who runs the trampolines next door. She holds a cocktail frankfurt between bright red nails. She examines it closely before popping it into her mouth.

'I thought we did,' Marie says, trying to remain composed.

'But what's the cost of a business in the city?' Beatrice sneaks a look as she licks the mustard from her fingers.

Marie knows when she is being pumped. She shrugs and drifts away. Whenever she stops to chat, people look at her strangely. She feels like a freak on show. She's a woman on the loose, gone feral; alluring to some and threatening to all the rest. She's the one who never fitted in, the one the locals tolerated for Ruben's sake. Acid remarks seem to hang in the air around her. She's the 'selfish wife' who has taken advantage of her husband's indulgence, and been seduced by life in the city.

Bernie from the Continental is reaching across for a snack and saying something to her. She leans closer, trying to catch his words. She can see his mouth moving but all she can hear is a man right behind her saying something about women and apes. A hot flush travels up her body. She wills herself not to turn around. She is nodding at Bernie but hearing nothing. Her head is full of the other conversation. There's a gust of laughter and then a sudden hush as the man realises that Marie is close by.

Marie excuses herself. She heads back to the kitchen, desperately searching the room for a pair of friendly eyes. Hannah notices the strain on her friend's face and gives Marie a wave. Across at the bar Ruben is sipping green beer. Slumped on his elbows he watches his wife as she edges her way through the crowd. Hannah concentrates on collecting glasses and passing around food, always keeping busy. She can't afford to contemplate the tangle of currents that flow beneath the chatter. All night she has been checking the crowd and wondering when Jake will show.

As Marie disappears out the back, Hannah's eyes stray towards the door. Jake has just come through with Anton. He stands slightly apart from the rest like he doesn't really want to be there. His face looks chiselled. His hair's been cropped close to his head like he's about to take a vow. It's the way he wanted her to cut it. All the waves are gone. With guarded eyes he waits in the farthest corner, while Anton goes for the drinks.

Hannah is at the bar on the other side of the room. She's just behind Anton when she hears his order and can't resist a sharp laugh. A lemon squash and a dry ginger ale. Anton turns on her with his lazy smile.

'Something funny?'

'Your drinks,' she says, her lips curled. She holds his gaze. 'They could really do some damage.' She'd never known Jake to drink anything softer than beer.

'Cutt-ing,' he drawls softly. He studies her for a moment. 'Don't blame me for your problems. Jake does what Jake wants. Anyway, why all the drama? He tells me that nothing much ever happened. It was no big deal, he said. Must be all in your head.'

Hannah stares at him. She is too stunned to speak. The glasses on the tray she's holding start to rattle. Amid the noise and confusion she casts her thoughts back over the summer and struggles to recall a moment or incident that would disprove Anton's claim. But there's a cloud of uncertainty hanging over it all.

Can she believe what Anton says? In a daze she moves off through the crowd still holding the tray of drinks. She has to find out for herself. She makes her way across to the other side of the room. Jake is watching her approach and glancing at the door as though he would like to bolt. Then he suddenly steps forward and stands right beside her as she gives away the last glass of wine.

'Too late,' she says looking at the empty tray.

'Anton's getting me something.'

'I know. A lemon squash.'

Jake laughs half-heartedly. 'No piss before a surf.'

Hannah remembers the night of the pictures, sitting in his car at the Back Beach before they ended up in bed. His talk of the moon and of surfing at night. Surely that had been a special night, in spite of Jake's storming out. Surely something *had* happened that night. And what about the weeks that followed? The days in the water together and the evenings after work. They weren't just in her head.

Jake is telling her they're going to Quarantine. Anton has got them a boat. With a south-easterly blowing it'll be the only break that'll work. Then he stops abruptly as though there's nothing more to be said. There's no room in his mind for anything else but the hours ahead. Hannah recognises the mood. She would get like that before an exam. So focused on what had to be done that nothing else mattered.

'I just spoke to Anton. He told me something you said about us. That there was no "us".'

'I don't know what he means. I didn't say that.'

'Say what?'

'That nothing happened.'

'What did you say?'

His voice is resigned. He seems suddenly sad. 'I can't remember, Hannah. It's too late now.'

She can see there's no point going on. She should've known she wouldn't get answers.

To her surprise, Jake leans forward and gives her a quick, fierce hug.

'Time to shoot through,' he says, as Anton approaches.

Hannah watches them say their goodbyes to Ruben and Marie before they disappear into the night.

Jake blows on a pile of twigs that are starting to crackle as the paper catches and envelops them in flame. As the fire takes hold he adds larger pieces of kindling that they've collected from the foreshore, and driftwood from the beach. Jake stands by the pit feeding the flames and dodging the smoke that keeps changing direction with unexpected gusts of wind. Anton emerges into the halo of light with another bundle scavenged from the Quarantine Station which lies obscured in blackness behind them. Soon the circle of light grows strong enough to give flickering glimpses of the old limestone hospital skirted by a wide verandah and the squat, roughly built hut that was once used as a mortuary. Jake has explored the old buildings many times before, and seen the stone slab with its deep grooves to drain the fluids while the post-mortem was in progress. Sometimes he'd think about the people who'd ended up here after making the long journey. In those crowded, disease-ridden hulks in search of a new life. He knew what it meant to travel halfway across the world in the hope of escaping the past. And he knew that it wasn't that simple. The past was a black hole that kept sucking you back into it. It was like an undertow you had to stop resisting in the hope that when it had finished dragging you down, the wave would pitch you out again.

Jake can hear the sea all around in the darkness. Occasionally the moon breaks through the clouds and hits the peeling wave. Its glittering underbelly flashes in horizontal streaks. Then comes the final heave as it spreads itself on the sand.

Anton scans the sky and when it is clear enough, they add extra fuel to the fire and then make their way to the water.

Marcus is dreaming of a giant wall of water rising out of the sea. He's watching it from above, as though suspended in the sky. The wave rears up and is poised to swallow the earth when something catches his eye. A tiny figure is paddling out to catch it. Removed from the impending danger, Marcus peers closer, wondering who would attempt such a crazy feat. As the wave towers over the land, ready for the final collision, Marcus sees the surfer's face and lets out a strangled cry.

He wakes in a sweat, his heart going like a train. Outside his bedroom window, the windchime is clamoring madly. The south-easterly has shifted around to the west and is blowing up to a gale.

Unable to go back to sleep he decides to take a walk.

When Anton bursts through the door of the cafe at two o'clock, Ruben, Marie and Hannah are in the final stages of clearing up. Anton's wetsuit drips water on the tiles. He brings with him the unruly tang of the sea. He is shivering so hard that for a while he can't speak.

'Where's Marcus? Does anyone know where he is?'

They look at him dumbly.

'Well?' he screams.

His rising panic fills the room. Hannah rushes at him and demands to know what's wrong. Anton looks at her, bewildered. Marie can see that he's in shock and probably on the verge of collapse. She guides him into a chair and sends Hannah for a blanket.

They have to contact Marcus, he says. Anton and Jake were surfing Quarantine when Jake went missing. They were sitting on their boards waiting for a set. Anton was keeping an eye on the fire to make sure they hadn't lost their bearings. When he turned to tell Jake they were drifting, he discovered that he was alone. The police had started searching the area but no one could get hold of Marcus.

The search vessel heaves through the darkness. It takes a wide arc toward the grey outline of the jetty at Quarantine. Hannah gulps in the cool air streaming past. With her stomach churning she is finding it hard to breathe. Beside her, Marcus is on the radio to the army barracks confirming their position. She listens to the crackling, syncopated voices and is amazed by their mechanical calm. Every frenetic burst of static ends with the word 'over'.

The motor is switched off and the launch bumps against the pylons. She climbs out quickly, lurches forward and throws up. She wipes her mouth and feels Marcus's hand on her back.

'Slow breaths,' he is saying in his deep, cracked voice. 'In and out.'

Hannah straightens up. They've been joined by two policemen who have been searching the Quarantine Station in case Jake made it back to the shore. On the beach they found the still warm coals of a dug-out fire and further down the coast toward the barracks, Anton's dinghy had been washed up on the rocks. Apart from two pairs of footsteps leading into the water, and one pair leading out, there were no other signs.

Hannah and Marcus climb back on the launch and pull away from the jetty, the bow smacking against waves as they plough toward the Heads. Aimlessly, Hannah flicks her torch across the water. Tiny creatures flitter through the wedge of light and are gone.

Beyond the protected bay they strike the heavy swell of the Rip. As they get closer to the open ocean, the rhythm of the boat begins to change. Instead of skimming across the surface it plunges into the deepening troughs and the engine begins to labour. Apart from the flash of a red light on the far shore, Hannah can see almost nothing. The horizon is obscured by the bumpy outline of cresting waves. The boat, which had seemed earlier like a substantial craft, now feels like something a child might make from paper. Something that could be overturned by the slightest gust. What it's like out there on a surfboard is too much to imagine. The chopping waves all around her have walled in her thoughts.

The boat thuds heavily against the waves sending jets of spray flying over the glass and into their faces. Now they are feeling the full force of the south-westerly gale. Marcus grips the wheel, his eyes fixed straight ahead. Water streams down his cheeks but he makes no effort to wipe them. His face is marble and glazed with pain. His body is there beside her, but his mind is somewhere else. Hannah watches him, knowing nothing she can say will comfort him. It's too late for that. There's nothing either of them can do but focus on the darkness ahead.

Other search vessels are buzzing up from behind and fanning out in different directions, but it's hard to believe that any of them will do much good. As they drone off into the distance, they sound as ineffectual as flies.

Jake keeps his eyes fixed on the square-rigged sailing ship, ablaze with fairy lights on the eastern horizon. Between lulls in the waves, gusts of music and laughter cross the distance with surprising ease. As shooting stars and water-falls of light explode above the anchored ship, Jake keeps paddling against the out-going tide. When he shuts his eyes and listens, the revellers seem close by, close enough to spot him and sound the alarm, or launch a rescue themselves. But when he opens his eyes again, the ship has grown much smaller and he has drifted out of range.

The moon shrinks as it rises into the sky. The fire on the beach at the Quarantine Station has been snuffed out by the wind. The tide is running faster and he knows that he's tiring himself by trying to resist. He calculates the time it will take before he's ejected into the open ocean—if he can survive the Rip itself. Probably an hour is all he's got. If it were simply a matter of enduring the cold he would easily make it. But the wind has whipped up the swell and things will only grow worse as he's sucked toward Bass Strait.

How could this have happened after all their careful plans? Months of talk and mapping the tide patterns, waiting for the right wind and swell. They had it down to the smallest detail. All day they'd worn dark glasses to keep their night vision sharp. The forecast hadn't predicted a gale, but there was more to it than the wind. There was something about the current that they hadn't struck before. What had happened to slack water, the lull between the tides?

Around the time he got separated from Anton, it had clouded over again making it difficult to see. The wind had also picked up and Jake's cries got blasted away. He lost sight of their dinghy and it was only when he tried paddling back to the pier, that he noticed the grip of the tide. To his surprise he'd been dragged into the shipping channel marked out by red and green lights. Once he found himself in the deep water, he was beyond reach of the breaking waves that might have propelled him toward the shore.

The pillar of the lighthouse on the far headland is getting closer. The outgoing tide seems to be taking him to the opposite shore. But Jake knows that it sweeps suddenly back as it travels out through the Rip and then god knows what happens. Half-heartedly, he waves at the red beacon that signals the out-going tide. He thinks of the radars that monitor the tankers and other international craft travelling through the heads. On a school excursion once he'd visited the sea pilots' station and seen the flickering maps that chart the constant traffic. The pilots could pick up a ship and track its course before radio contact was made. But a tanker looked no bigger than a pulsing dot. Something the size of a surfboard wouldn't even register on the screen.

As he's bundled toward the Strait, he watches with great longing the ghostly beauty of the Peninsula's receding coastline. Occasionally a fist of tea-tree erupts from the rolling scrub. In a clearing at the Point, the crumbling walls of the fort reflect the pale moonlight. The cliff tumbles to a crescent of beach. Off to the right, the Southern Cross is hanging low in the sky, almost upside down, as though dragged low by its weight. Or perhaps by the tiredness that's also dragging at him. The constant struggle to keep his board, to watch out for the waves that piggy-back the one in front and pack a double punch. It has started to wear him down.

Where the Peninsula ends, the water chops even more violently as the bay and Strait collide. In the growing cold and confusion, as he fights to stay afloat, his mind snags on odd details like the bombed-out buildings he used to play in as a child, and Hannah waving at him from the pier and Marcus kneeling in the dunes, his face obscured by his hat. He wishes his father would look up and speak to him, but Marcus keeps his head well down as though afraid to meet his son's eyes.

The horizon disappears as Jake sinks between two peaks, and when he rises out of the trough, something makes him cry out loud. He has only seen it once before, and that was from the land. A wall of white water breaking from Head to Head. A solid wave choking the mouth of the bay.

There is no time to think. No time to even panic before a massive slap knocks him sideways like a building has collapsed on his head. He grips the rails and gasps through the foam and spray. There's a violent jerk, then his leg rope goes slack as the water buries him with its weight. The only thing he knows is that he must keep hold of his board. He wraps his legs around it and wrestles with the wave. The pressure increases as the fibreglass buoys him up while the water forces him down.

The world has never seemed so remote.

Just as the board is about to spear from under him, he feels a sudden ignition, a surging forward, as the wave erupts and spits him from the Rip in the hardest ride of his life.

It takes some time before Jake can bring himself to loosen his grip on his board. He has held it so tight he can feel the shape of his hands imprinted in the fibreglass. He flings the water from his eyes and tries to get his bearings. He is outside the Heads. The wall of white is behind him. The swell is heavy but regular. He knows its rhythm well. The deadly turbulence is gone.

Although he is approaching familiar waters everything looks strange. Down the back of the Peninsula he can make out Cheviot and Spooks and the pale streak of the Long Beach. He can see the milky breakers leaving trails of lace down the coastline that reaches all the way to Cape Schanck. He can see the bare rump of the sand dunes and bush rising up behind them and the occasional clump of lights from houses along the cliffs. And he can see the battered face of the Sphinx taking the brunt of it all.

Jake surveys the whole coast with amazement. Everything is still as it was. It hasn't been washed away. He lowers his head to his board and closes his eyes. The sea rocks him, rising and falling, urging him to rest. His arms slip off the sides and hang like seaweed in the current. Water seems to be seeping through his pores. As he sinks deeper, there's the faintest high-pitched hum travelling up from below. Like a mosquito in his ear drawing him back from sleep. His head jolts up. He blinks and looks around.

There is no boat.

The cliffs of Cheviot are rearing up on his left. The wind is stiff at his back. He must do something or he will drift on to the rocks. He swings his board around to face the Sphinx and with what little strength he has left, he begins to slowly paddle through the grainy, pre-dawn light.

SWIMMING IN SILK
Darren Williams

Winner of the *Australian*/Vogel Literary
Award

'Highly evocative . . . what captivates is the
landscape.'

Jill Kitson

'The writing is an absolute pleasure, creating
an atmosphere that draws the reader in.'

Marele Day

Brilliant skies, sudden storms, black nights
and a ramshackle house that is disintegrating
into the rainforest. Sheltering from their
pasts, Cliff, Susan, Daniel and Jade
experience a few oddly idyllic days and
nights together in the small coastal town two
of them call home and to which the others
have returned.

Swimming in Silk is an extraordinarily
evocative and sensual novel about the
mysterious and intricate relationship between
people, the elements, and the land in which
they live.

1 86373 849 5

BRACELET HONEYMYRTLE
Judith Fox

Shortlisted in the *Australian*/Vogel Literary Award

'Wonderfully sustained . . . the sense of fulfilment achieved in simple reflection is marvellous.'

Jill Kitson

'A splendid, moving book.'

Andrew Reimer

Annie Grace is an old woman. She tends her garden, and cares for a baby, her great great-niece, Kimberley. It is a quiet life.

Born into a strict Christian family in Sydney at the start of the century, Annie contends with an overbearing mother and a harsh religion. Yet something stirs under the starch of faith. Annie finds a friend late in life and discovers a passion for living to equal her passion for gardening. In her sixties, Annie confronts her mother.

This is the story of one woman's struggle to lay claim to her own life. And within the seemingly narrow contours of family and church and garden, Annie discovers that it is, after all, a big life.

1 86373 850 9

A MORTALITY TALE
Jay Verney

Shortlisted in the *Australian*/Vogel Literary
Award

'Like flood, heat, age and guilt this book
creeps up on you—forcing you to take
notice.'

Jennifer Rowe

One rainy night Vincent Cusack appears,
briefly, lit up for one final, fatal moment in
the headlights of Carmen Molloy's car.
Carmen is unquestionably an honourable
woman, yet is able to drive on home and to
be apparently shocked and saddened by news
the next day of Vincent's untimely death.

In an exceptionally witty, perceptive and
challenging literary debut, Jay Verney teases
readers with fascinating 'What if?' questions
as Carmen hosts Vincent's wake, avoids
police questioning, battles a chorus of
internal voices—and promises herself she can
get away with the most disturbing of crimes.

1 86373 669 7

BEYOND BERLIN
Penelope Nelson

'swift-moving and energetic . . . Nelson is behind her stage and in control.'
Sydney Morning Herald

For Libby Milroy, 1970 is a year of political protest, sexual obsession and self-discovery. Arriving in Berlin at the height of the international student rebellion, she is intoxicated by the excitement that the city seems to promise. So much so that she ignores the warning signs as people close to her move from street protests to the politics of terrorism.

Twenty years later, she is asked to confront the loyalties and dilemmas of her youth and be ready to make some tough decisions about the future.

1 86373 847 9

SOLSTICE
Matt Rubinstein

Shortlisted in the *Australian*/Vogel Literary Award

'An exuberant inside look at Australian youth culture . . . Amazingly, a first novel in Vikram Seth's demotic mode.'

Judith Rodriguez

'An Oz Midsummer Nights Dream, witty tender and erudite.'

Rhyll McMaster

Twenty-four hours in mid-summer Adelaide. A city seething with vitality at a microscopic level. A vibrant patchwork of individuals, colourful and unique. Twenty-four hours of love lost, and found in instant passion, or travel and adventure, captured and transformed in verse which leaps, and tricks to race and stop the clock.

The characters? In their talented and tormented twenties: their stories told in a beautiful and different way.

A brilliant literary debut that will inevitably be likened to Vikram Seth's *Golden Gate*—and is as vivid and refreshing.

1 86373 723 5

THE MULE'S FOAL
Fotini Epanomitis

Winner of the *Australian*/Vogel Literary
Award

'*The Mule's Foal* has entered my dreams.'
> *Sydney Morning Herald*

'An extraordinary, enchanting and beautiful
book . . . Epanomitis' effortless control over
her narrative, the grave, rhythmic quality of
her language, and the sense of profound
human truths within the fantastic which gives
this novel its power to entrance.'
> *Canberra Times*

In one despairing moment Theodosios
abandons his wife and gorilla child and then
spends a lifetime trying to get them back.
But what's a lifetime in a place like this?

Here nothing belongs to you—not even your
grief. People steal your letters and gossip
your thoughts before you've spoken them.
And when they're desperate—and at some
point everyone is desperate—they go to the
whorehouse . . .

From the centre of chaos, Mirella, the
ancient whore, finds a calm place to tell this
unforgettable, timeless tale.

1 86373 454 6